Tamika
The Queen of X

Eugene Rookwood

Dexcel Publishing * Indianapolis, Indiana

Tamika
The Queen of X

ISBN 978-0-9704015-3-3

Printed in the United States of America

This story and all episodes of the Trilogy of X is one hundred percent erotic fiction. If any of the characters or situations seems oddly familiar...it is only because outrageous behavior is not original!

...Eugene Rookwood

Chapter one

Back in the day when rhythm and blues flowed freely from brand new eight-track players it was an agonizing, blood-curling scream that put me on the emergency mission of driving a very pregnant Ruth Ann Martin to the hospital. It was an experience I never forgot because she screamed all the way and as I knew absolutely nothing about child birthing, I was scared to death. Since I knew the lady very well I hung around the hospital for several hours until she gave birth to her fourth child. Ruth Ann was a thirty-one year old unmarried black woman who, for whatever reason, never identified the child's father and he never identified himself. She named the child Tamika Rochelle Martin and in a few days mother and child left the hospital and went home to Nelson Park. Nelson Park was a cluster of public housing apartment buildings. Okay honestly, Nelson Park was "THE PROJECTS".

Kids grow up fast in the projects and Tamika was no exception. She was a plain and kinda homely looking child, not at all pretty or really even attractive. Nonetheless, she was very perceptive and sassy with a

disarming smile that charmed men and women alike. Tamika must have taken after her father, because she is nothing like her mama. Ruth Ann Martin is truly one overbearing bitch. Loud, ignorant, demanding, got to have her way, got to have the last word, and knows every damn thing. She goes through men like paper towels, throwing or chasing away most, re-using some, keeping none. Ruth Ann collects welfare and hangs out in her favorite watering hole when she can. She smokes too much, drinks too much, does drugs too much and spends too little time with her children.

I know all this because my name is Winston Littles and I live in the same building. I collect disability from the Army, fix cars on the side and try to mind my own business. I first met Ruth Ann while I was moving into Nelson Park. I was single, fresh out of the Army and had just turned twenty years old, while Ruth Ann was twenty-nine and had three children. She stopped me in the hallway to let me know that I turned her on and she was ready to prove it. I took the bait and since that encounter I've had and been had by Ruth Ann way too many times so now I try real hard to avoid her. But, regardless of the adults the projects is the domain of the children and because of that sometimes annoying fact I've watched Tamika grow up.

Parenting wasn't a high priority for Ruth Ann. She was gone from home for long periods of time while her children would freely wander around the projects. Starting when Tamika was about four years old she always seemed to be hanging around while I was working on a car. She didn't say much but every time I turned around there she was, perched in one place or another with this big smile on her face. When she got a

little older and found out I had color TV she would knock on my door then hide in the hallway. When the door opened she would make a mad dash inside my apartment then curl up in my lap or on the floor in front of the TV. Several times I just left her there and went on about my business. Her charm and intellect grew as quickly as she did and soon it seemed everyone genuinely liked this child and wanted to please her. Everybody that is, except for her mama. Them two never did get along. Ruth Ann couldn't deal with this child's intellect and as far as I could see never really tried.

As I said kids grow up fast in the projects and Tamika was ahead of the pack. Because her mama showed little interest she never failed to bring me her school report card. She was a student that showed lots of potential but got high marks only in the few subjects that interested her. Due to a lack of guidance, parental support and poor attendance, Tamika like a lot of the kids in Nelson Park barely made passing grades and were years behind their peers in the larger world. But unlike most of the other kids Tamika was enterprising. Starting at about age eight she set up shop in the apartment courtyard and sold bouquets of "sunshine flowers" better know as dandelions. A couple of years later I noticed her doing brisk business selling lemonade. I was impressed until I learned the lemonade was heavily spiked with Ruth Ann's gin.

By the time she was around twelve or so Tamika put together a list of phone numbers of all the single women in Nelson Park then sold copies of the list to interested gentlemen. Because of its success the list was expanded to include a brief profile describing the dating habits of each lady. The new list was priced three times

higher than the first one and sold even better until a few of the ladies on the list paid Tamika a visit. She stopped selling the list but her spirit was undaunted.

Tamika was full of life and by fourteen was one hot frustrated little mama and knew it. I didn't allow her to come up to my apartment anymore...her tail was too hot and I don't fuck children. Still she would catch me working on a car behind the building and try to do some heavy flirting. What I thought about her body development seemed important to her.

"Are my titties getting bigger, Uncle Wint?" she would ask. "Do you like my booty? Does it turn you on? I got hair growing between my legs, want to see it?"

My reply was usually the same, "Carry yo little young ass away from here girl. I don't need to be bothered by you right now."

She always replied, "I'll go. But...not for long!"

No matter what I said, when I chased her off, she would always smile that killer smile and say, "I'll go. But...not for long!" Once I asked her just what the hell "not for long" is supposed to mean anyway? She looked right into my eyes with a devilish yet very serious look and replied, "Uncle Wint you know exactly what I mean. Sooner or later...it's on with you and me."

"Get outta here!" I responded.

"I'll go. But...not for long!" she warned as she left.

By the time she was sixteen she was complaining mightily about young boys. "All they wanna do is fuck and they don't even know how Uncle Wint. I want me a man who knows HOW to make love so he can teach me. I want to really get all the way into it. You know what I mean, Uncle Wint? I'm sexy and I want to be like Keisha. She knows how to do it all and is fucking everybody!"

Tamika declared.

"Naw...come on now...hell she's only a year older than you ain't she?" I asked with growing suspicion.

"She's Nuggy's age, two years older than me, and one night she got fucked up and did everybody," Tamika insisted.

"What you mean did everybody?" I questioned.

"She did both of my brothers and hers too!" Tamika giggled.

"Girl!" I responded. "You know I don't have no time for a bunch of lies."

"It's the truth Uncle Wint...really! Nobody was home at first but me and Nuggy and we was dancing when Keisha stopped by. She was already high and had a bag of weed. So I sat down and started rolling some joints while Keisha and Nuggy started slow dancing. When the song ended Nuggy started talking shit then laid down on the couch and swore Keisha had made his thing so hard it was about to explode. So Keisha went and stood over him. She unbuttoned her blouse and wasn't wearing a bra so her titties just fell out and she teased Nuggy with them. Nuggy couldn't stand it I guess so he opened his pants and pulled his thing out. Keisha winked her eye at me then said, "Ohhh look at that...you want to see me do your brother Tamika?"

"I said yeah. So Keisha bent over and rubbed her titties all over Nuggy's thing and then put it in her mouth and sucked on it. Oooo...Nuggy freaked, he screamed and grabbed Keisha's head...then he came real hard. He was bouncing up and down...hee-hee, he was. Keisha pumped his thang with her hand, then stood on the couch, right over Nuggy and said..."go find you a

girl...BOY! You ain't ready for a WOMAN!"

Nuggy just grinned and stared up Keisha's dress. Right after that Nuggy smoked a joint then left but Keisha was totally loaded. She told me she wished I was a boy cause she would suck it and fuck me all night long. She even promised to teach me how to suck one. Then she said she was going to do me. She's got big soft titties; they nice and she started squeezing and rubbing them. She can even suck her own nipples Uncle Wint. That's what she was doing when Sam and Drey came in. They almost caught us and you know, I really don't think Keisha would have cared if they did. I was pissed off. I really wanted Keisha to do me and they spoiled my opportunity. So I said I was going to bed and left the room but I stayed were I could see them without being spotted. Keisha lit a joint and just left her blouse hanging wide open. Drey said something about Keisha being really fucked-up then he said something about her big pretty titties and she went right over and put one into his mouth. Drey was sitting on the arm of the couch and he sucked both her titties real good while she was running her fingers all through his hair and shit. Sam said, "Hey lay off motherfucker that's your sister!"

And Drey said, "No shit?"

Keisha laughed and said, "Yeah...no shit! Come here cousin." She turned around and sat on Drey grinding her butt into his lap while he leaned back trying to get his thing right under her. Keisha handed Sam the joint, loosened his belt then pulled his thing out of his shorts. It was hard and she stroked it up and down and teased him. Then she said, "You want me to suck it, huh cuz?"

Sam said, "Hell yeah Keish baby, do it!"

But she didn't. She stroked it a few more times, then stood up and took off all her clothes. She told Drey and Sam to take off their pants and shorts then she ordered Sam to lie back on the couch. When he did she sat on his lap then spread her pussy with her fingers and guided his thing right into her. After that she leaned forward, grabbed Drey's big thing and put it in her mouth. Oooo I couldn't believe it Uncle Wint! For a minute they didn't move then Keisha began to suck and fuck both of them. I got really excited because I had never seen anything like that. Then all of a sudden Drey jerked his thing out of Keisha's mouth and came on her titties. And just about the same time Sam pushed her off and shot his cum on her butt. Then Drey flopped back into the big chair and Sam laid back on the couch and closed his eyes but Keisha was really pissed and she hollered at them, "You motherfuckers ain't shit, two fucking minutes and bang!"

Sam said, "Sorry Keish baby yo pussy just too hot."

And Keisha said, "Don't give me that shit! I want to fuck! Get it back up." She tried sucking Sam then Drey again but neither one of them could get hard again so Keisha washed up real quick then put her clothes on but kept on bitching. "Fuck you Drey. Twenty-four years old and can't even keep a hard-on. And you worse Sam yo ass just turned twenty-one. Shit...I'm gonna give this pussy to a real man."

Sam said, " Keisha, you a fucking nympho, an eighteen year old nympho."

So Keisha said, "Yo ass Sam, you just can't fuck BOY!"

And Sam goes... "BOY?"

And she hollered, "THAT'S WHAT I SAID! You fuck like a BOY! Come on Drey get your shit on, let's go home...COME ON!"

And Drey goes, "All right all right! Goddamn! What's the hurry...shit!" Then he struggled into his clothes and followed Keisha out the door. "

"A couple weeks later Drey's mama, Aunt Norma, had a card party and me and mama and Nuggy and Jewel was all over there. I went back to Drey's bedroom and he closed the door and had me lean against it. Then he pulled my panties down and started finger fucking me. I was really hot and wanting to do it but he was having trouble trying to get it in. His thing was really big and I was kind of tight so he was struggling and grunting. Then just as I was starting to feel that big thing really push into me he came and came really hard. Then he pulled it out and cum dripped out of me. Drey slapped my booty and told me to go clean up. But I wasn't through; in fact I had hardly got started. I asked him what the fuck he meant. I wanted to do it. He said, "We did do it and I done skint my dick on yo tight ass so beat it. Get the fuck on outta here." That's exactly what he said; he's such a sorry ass! Then he called my mama and told her I was bothering him and she made me come back to the living room. "

"That's why I know LaKeisha is right. She handled Sam and Drey at the same time and she got two boyfriends. One of them is older than you are Uncle Wint. She said he taught her how to really get down and they do everything all the time. She's always bragging about her sweet old meat. But I don't care about her bragging cause I got you...and you got the sweetest old meat there is...tee-hee-hee-hee," Tamika giggled.

"You mighty sure of yourself. What you know about any of that?" I demanded.

"I heard mama bragging about you. She said you was one man that like to fuck all night long and had the sweetest piece of black meat she ever tasted. She said she would be tingling for days after a night with you," Tamika responded.

"Did she tell you that?" I questioned.

"Naw, you kidding! I overheard her talking to Wanda."

"When?" I inquired.

"Long time ago, anyway that don't matter. I know what I want," Tamika insisted.

"Yeah right. Well too bad little girl, you too damn young and I don't fuck children," I advised.

"Bullshit! Sooner or later Uncle Wint," Tamika responded. "Sooner or later your thang is mine...can I see it?"

"Go away!" I demanded.

"Uh-huh...I'll go. But...not for long Uncle Wint! Not for long," Tamika promised.

Chapter two

About this time Wilona Freeman with her three children and her live-in boyfriend Lester moved into the Nelson Park projects. Wilona was a private duty nurse's aide who worked both on and off the record and Lester was a hospital orderly. Darnell was Wilona's only son and oldest child. He was about eighteen and without doubt a total sex freak in the making. One night not long after they moved in, I was sitting out back on the fire escape smoking a joint and saw Darnell come into his bedroom and stare into a full-length mirror for several minutes. He took off his clothes then started playing with himself. In short order he had a full-blown hard-on and was busy jacking off when the door flew open.

"What the hell you doing Darnell?" Lester demanded.

"What the hell does it look like?" Darnell shot back.

"It looks like you are becoming a man," Lester said as he came into the room closing the door behind him. "I could hear you gruntin all the way out in the living room."

"So what, ain't nobody home...and what you

keep looking at?" Darnell questioned.

"As I said, it looks like you are becoming a man, a beautiful strong black MAN!" Lester replied.

"Think so...really?" Darnell asked hopefully.

"No doubt about it! Take your hands away so I can see all of you!" Lester demanded.

"Hey you a faggot ain't you Lester? I knowed it the first day mama bring yo ass home! You is! Ain't you?" Darnell questioned.

"Darnell?" Lester grinned. "Boy you don't have to be a faggot to admire a gorgeous sexy body. Hey boy, the good lord put some ugly motherfuckers on this earth and he put some fine ones here too, male and female. If I only admired one sex then I would be cheated out of admiring the other, so I admire any fine motherfucker when I see one...and right now I'm admiring you. Turn around and let me look at your tender young ass. My, my...look at you...handsome face, well defined chest, nice shoulders, rippled stomach, narrow waist, a tight round bubble ass that's just wonderful and a big-big black dick...shit you beautiful boy."

"Fuck you Lester you made me lose my hard-on. I'm getting dressed!" Darnell snapped.

"Wait...wait just a minute...ole Lester made you lose it, ole Lester will help you get it back." Lester reached out and began massaging Darnell's semi-hard dick.

"Ooo sheeit...you better stop Lester...that feels good," Darnell moaned.

"It's going to feel a whole lot better Darnell but this shit's between you and me...understand?" Lester demanded.

"Yeah, yeah no problem," Darnell sighed.

"I mean it motherfucker. If your mama finds out about this I'm gonna fuck you up!" Lester warned. "You like that...don't cha?"

"Uh huh... don't stop!" Darnell pleaded.

Lester dropped to his knees and began to massage Darnell's dick and balls with both hands. In the short time it took to get the young boy hard and throbbing, ole Lester was sweating and starting to slobber. He could stand it no longer and slowly slid Darnell's dick into his anxious mouth.

Darnell tensed and jerked from the intense pleasure of having his dick really sucked for the first time in his young life. "Whew...shit baby...suck that dick...ooo shit...do it! Goddamn Lester...umm..." he gasped. His young dick wasn't quite five inches long and Lester sucked all of it with enthusiasm, his hands tightly gripping Darnell's ass. Fully excited, Darnell grabbed Lester's head and pumped his hips into the older man's face.

Lester was almost as excited as Darnell. He had wanted to taste this young dick since he first moved in and had never failed to sneak a look at a naked Darnell whenever he could. He began sucking in tight wet strokes as his common-law stepson started to cum. Lester then swallowed that young dick as far as he could get it and moaned while Darnell pumped hot semen deep into his throat. They couldn't stop, Darnell finally stopped cumming but his dick was still hard and for both of them it felt too good to stop. Darnell began to fuck Lester's mouth in a furious rhythm while Lester smacked and moaned, until Darnell abruptly withdrew his dick then shot a fresh load of cum into Lester's open

mouth.

Finally Lester stood up taking Darnell's dick in his hand and milking the last bit of cum from it. "Remember, this is between you and me kid," he reminded before letting go.

"Yeah...yeah...damn that was good! But next time I'm gonna fuck you in yo faggot ass," Darnell threaten.

"You might, but I don't think you could handle it even if I showed you how," Lester replied.

"Hey you really been fucked in the ass Lester?" Darnell questioned.

"I gotta get ready for work. See you later Darnell," Lester responded with a smile.

"Answer the question punk, you been fucked in the ass or not?" Darnell demanded.

"Why, huh? Why you want to know anyway?" Lester shot back.

"Cause you a punk...you a fag if you been fucked in yo ass everybody knows that!" Darnell insisted.

"Everybody don't know shit," Lester snapped. "I sleep with your mama don't I. Some people are lucky enough to enjoy all kinds of sex and that don't make them no fag or no nothing...but people."

"So I guess you enjoy all kinds of sex...huh?" Darnell questioned.

"If it is any of your goddamn business yes I do!"

"Does mama know that?" Darnell asked.

"I told you this is between you and me," Lester warned in a threatening voice.

"You gonna let me fuck you in the ass?" Darnell pleaded.

"We'll talk, but right now I gotta get to work

before I'm late. By the way, I meant what I said about you becoming a beautiful black man and your dick is simply delicious...later," Lester concluded as he left the room.

For much of his young life Darnell had been trying to fuck any thing or person he could. His luck hadn't been all bad but it couldn't be called good either. He had cum in his pants, fucked his pillow, his sister's dolls and a watermelon he and some friends fixed up. He even tried fucking one of his buddies in the ass with no luck. Occasionally he got a chance at real pussy but he came so quickly that he never really got to fuck. Since he could remember his favorite pastime has always been playing with himself and he had managed to get his young penis stuck in a juice bottle, toilet paper core and vacuum cleaner nozzle among other places. But now that Lester, his mama's old man had sucked him off, Darnell felt a new confidence, aggressiveness and a sense of himself that he liked. Over the next few days he could think of nothing else. He truly wanted Lester to suck him off again but the thought of fucking Lester in the ass made his dick so hard his balls ached. Lester was acting as though nothing had happened and that was driving Darnell crazy with raw lust.

Wilona worked days mostly while Lester worked the second shift and sometimes the third so Darnell's opportunities were limited. For three days in a row he hurried straight home from school hoping to catch Lester before he left for work, but each time Lester was not there. So on the fourth day Darnell walked his two sisters to their school as usual then went straight back home. He was only one year behind in school and determined to graduate but right now school could wait.

Today he was going to fuck Lester in his ass. When he got home he went straight to his bedroom, undressed then went looking for Lester. He searched the whole apartment but Lester was not there. Darnell was truly pissed, his dick throbbed and disappointment ate at him. Dejected he decided to find something new in the house to fuck. He was standing naked in the kitchen and had just selected a large jar of jelly as the next victim for his raging hard-on when he heard the front door open and close. Darnell peeked into the living room and saw Lester coming toward the kitchen with a bag of groceries.

"Take off your clothes bitch!" he announced when Lester stepped through the kitchen door.

"Can I at least put these groceries up first?" Lester asked.

"Hurry up with it!" Darnell demanded. "I'm gonna shove this big dick all the way up yo fat yellah ass bitch!"

"That's a beautiful hard-on you got there big man," Lester complimented.

"Uh huh. You gonna feel all of it too! Now get outta them clothes!" Darnell ordered.

Lester quickly put the groceries away then headed to Darnell's bedroom leaving his clothes in a trail behind him. Darnell followed closely, his young hard-on bobbing in front of him.

"So you want to fuck this ass?" Lester questioned as he turned and clamped his mouth on Darnell's nipple. Darnell was taken aback, he didn't know his nipples were sensitive and having them sucked and licked on was a brand new thrill. Lester pushed Darnell onto his bed and began seriously sucking and licking the young

boy's chest and stomach. "You wanna just shove your dick up my ass or do you want me to show you how to really make love to a man?" Lester demanded.

"Make love to me sweet bitch," Darnell moaned.

"I'm gonna lick every inch of your sweet brown ass," Lester gasped as his tongue snaked its way across Darnell's body.

It was a completely new experience for Darnell and excited him like never before. He felt Lester's tongue on his neck, in his ears, on his cheek and chin. Lester licked his arms, even his armpits. Darnell loved it. Lester's hot tongue seemed to be everywhere at once. Darnell turned over and Lester licked his shoulders, his back, his legs, his cheeks, the crack of his ass, he even sucked Darnell's toes. Darnell's head was spinning and he was way beyond himself. He wanted Lester to put that hot tongue in his mouth so he could suck on it and feel Lester's mouth on his. He wondered what Lester's dick would feel and taste like. Suddenly a jolt of intense pleasure shot through him...Lester's tongue was stabbing his asshole. Lester's head bobbed up and down as his tongue went deeper and deeper into Darnell's virgin ass.

"Goddamn I'm gonna cum," Darnell moaned.

"Not yet sweet daddy," Lester replied as he repositioned Darnell then began sucking each one of his balls, before taking both of them into his mouth. He swirled his tongue around and around them while Darnell held tightly to his head. When Lester knew that his young lover couldn't take much more he sucked Darnell's hard aching dick into his mouth. Cum exploded from Darnell and Lester happily drank every drop then kept sucking until Darnell was completely dry

and no longer hard.

"Wow...wow!" Darnell gasped.

"Don't talk, just relax sweet daddy...relax...then I'll do you again," Lester purred as he moved up and lay beside his common-law stepson. He took Darnell into his arms and gently kissed him on the forehead several times while whispering, "Relax daddy relax."

Still floating, Darnell snuggled into Lester's embrace and closed his eyes. The non-stop excitement had drained him, yet he was finding a new thrill in the touch of their naked bodies pressed close together. In spite of himself Darnell soon fell asleep, awaking several hours later with a throbbing hard-on. But, Lester was gone and his sisters were home from school. *Damn!* Darnell thought, *I still ain't fucked that ass, but I'm gonna, so help me I'm gonna.*

Chapter three

It was only a matter of time before Tamika and Darnell met each other. When I saw them hanging out together I figured they had hooked up pretty close and quite frankly I was relieved. I've had more than enough of Tamika's hot, sassy young ass tempting me and from what I've seen, Darnell most certainly needed a ready young GIRL in his life. Tamika stopped bothering me for quite awhile just when I got real busy for a good spell. Don't know why but things just started to fall my way. Lots of folks around here were having small car problems. Small shit's my specialty, I only fix little shit. I don't mess around with no big car problems cause I'm disabled you know.

One day I was working under the hood of a car and thinking that on one hand I kind of miss Tamika's little spicy visits. But on the other hand I'm glad she don't come around anymore. No sooner than I looked up to get a wrench there she was. She looked different because she had on a short skirt and some kind of school sweater, which I am sorry I ever mentioned.

"This is my cheerleader outfit, Uncle Wint," she

explained.

"Congratulations! You a cheerleader now huh?" I commented.

"Hell naw, I tried out but I didn't get picked," Tamika pouted.

"Oh, I'm sorry baby I bet I know why they didn't pick you," I replied.

"Why?"

"Cause you so fine everybody would always be ignoring the other girls and looking at you," I advised.

"Ooo…talk shit Uncle Wint, you my man! Naw, the real reason I didn't get picked is cause they only wanted them high yellow bitches that look like white girls. But hey that's cool I got this outfit except I don't like the panties they are too thick," Tamika replied.

"Don't you have to give that back to the school?"

"All the other tryouts have to but I don't. I get to keep mine cause the gym teacher gave it to me. She felt me up for a long time then she told me to keep the outfit and to stay away from her," Tamika giggled.

"What kind of shit is that?" I questioned.

"I don't know!" Tamika replied. "She called me in after I didn't make the squad. She didn't have nothing to do with the tryouts. I was going to the locker room to change and she called me into her office. She said she thought I should have made the squad because I had a lot of enthusiasm. Then she said she would give me some pointers for next year and got behind me and started talking about posture and shit. She put her arms around me and started feeling on my stomach and below my titties and shit and I liked it so I put my hands on hers and just kinda laid back on her. Then she felt my titties and put her nose on my neck for a long time but

she wouldn't let me take my top off. Then she felt up my stomach and my thighs. She was breathing real hard and used both hands to feel up my pussy. It felt soo good, oooh shit Uncle Wint, I thought I was gonna pass out. She told me to lay back on her desk but she wouldn't let me take my panties off either. I told her I wanted to but she said no. She just pushed me back and rubbed her mouth on my pussy. I hate them cheerleader panties they so thick I couldn't feel that much. Anyway, I liked her hands on my pussy best, but she rubbed her mouth and nose on my pussy for a long time, then she turned her back to me and said, You better go." I asked why because I liked what we were doing. But she said, "No I want you to stay away from me, and if you promise to forget about this, I'll let you keep your cheerleader outfit, just make damn sure you never wear it to school. Anyway you wanna see me do some cheers Uncle Wint? Watch. Yea rah Bulldogs! Watch Uncle Wint, Yea rah Bulldogs. YEA RAH... BULLDOGS!!!"

"Hey girl! Set yo ass down!" I snapped. "You ain't got no pants on under that dress."

"I know Uncle Wint; I told you I don't like them." She hopped up on a nearby car and pulled her knees up to her chest. "This is what I really came round here to show you Uncle Wint," she teased.

"Girl cover yo self up, what the hells the matter with you?" I fumed.

"Come on Uncle Wint, you know this is your pussy, ha-ha," Tamika teased. "You know you want to poke it, don't you? Ha-ha."

"Look at you...just found yourself a nice new boyfriend and here you are acting up," I chastised.

Tamika hopped off the car. "What boyfriend?" she

questioned. "Who you talking about Uncle Wint?"

"Darnell, that's who! I seen ya'll hanging together."

"Darnell! HA!" Tamika snorted. "That boy is weird. You know he said his mama's boyfriend sucks his thang."

"Oh? And you two ain't been hanging out huh?"

"Yeah we friends but he can't fuck, he can't even get it in before he cums and he be wanting to fuck you in the butt and shit! Keisha don't like him cause he cummed on her dress. She say he's gonna be a fag. But he's alright for a friend. Drey wants to fuck Darnell in his butt and me and Keisha wanna watch, so we been talking him into it. He wants to but he scared. He thinks everybody will be calling him a fag. He said he wants to fuck and get fucked at the same time. I told you he's weird. I don't want to fuck him anyway. I know who I want and I want you right in here," Tamika advised.

"Good-bye Tamika," I concluded.

"Don't be like that Uncle Wint!" Tamika complained as she hopped back onto the car. "I ain't bothered you for a long time and I'm seventeen now. I'm on the pill and I got some rubbers too. I do...I got them at school. Everybody wants to fuck but you. All them old men mama bring home be talking shit and trying to feel me up. If I don't like them I tell mama and she goes off on they ass. I don't wanna fuck them though. I don't wanna fuck them old men that sit out front neither. They be trying to pinch my ass on the sly. All my life I ain't wanted but one thang in here and I'm gonna get it too. Look at my pussy Uncle Wint, ain't it pretty?"

"Yes Tamika, that pussy is real pretty. Now cover it up and go home!" I demanded.

"You starting to piss me off Uncle Wint," Tamika snapped then jumped off the car. "How much longer I gotta wait huh?"

"I don't know...forever!" I answered.

"Bullshit Uncle Wint! Nuh uh..." Tamika insisted. "I ain't waiting much longer you hear. It's gonna be sooner AND later. Come on Uncle Wint look at me! I'm ready...don't you want me? she demanded.

"Tamika...babygirl...now you know and I know that you are a fine young thing," I responded. "But you like my own...you need a boy more your own age. Don't get me wrong, on the face of things I would love to have you baby, but I'm damn near 40 years old and you just a kid. That shit would never work." I called myself letting her down easy.

"Oh it's gonna work Uncle Wint! I'm gonna make it work, you'll see," Tamika insisted.

"Oh yeah? Just how you gonna do that?" I questioned.

"You'll see Uncle Wint!" Tamika promised with a wide knowing smile. "You'll see."

Chapter four

Darnell *was living in quiet, frenzied* sexual heat when he met Tamika. She didn't really appeal to him but she had an unexplained power and pushed him into several sexual encounters. First she made him undress but he climaxed before getting all his clothes off and that pissed her off. Soon she discovered that she could just rub her ass against him and he would cum in his pants. When he did she would make him walk around all day with cum in his shorts. One day she made him cum in his shorts three times. His pants were stained and soaked but she made him walk around with her anyway. Darnell was embarrassed but secretly loved it.

Tamika took him to her cousin's house and LaKeisha was going to demonstrate how to sixty-nine. She had Darnell lay on the floor, took off her panties and climbed on top of him. She spread her legs over Darnell's head and rubbed her pussy on his face. Then opened his pants and started tugging at his dick. As soon as she got it free Darnell shot his load soiling LaKeisha's dress and she went nuts. It was then that she threatened to have Drey fuck Darnell in his ass. It was the first time anyone had seriously suggested fucking

his ass and hearing this made Darnell's asshole tingle and spasm. It was a frightening yet wonderful sensation he had never felt before and it made him uncomfortable. A couple days later when he came face-to-face with Drey he experienced that same feeling again. LaKeisha had told Drey he should fuck Darnell and Drey thought it was a good idea. He had enjoyed some boy pussy in the joint and was game for more but didn't think Darnell was really ready.

Tamika was intrigued with the idea. She wanted to see Darnell get fucked in his butt but Drey wasn't moving fast enough for her, so she introduced Darnell to a boy named Aaron White. Tamika had decided Aaron was gay because he didn't want to fuck her or any other girl she knew and she was right. Aaron hung around the high school locker room peeping at dicks and he dearly wanted to play with one.

Aaron and Darnell hit it right off. Within two days they were jacking each other off. At first they let Tamika watch but soon made plans to meet in private. They agreed to skip school, meet at Aaron's house and go beyond jacking each other off. But on the morning he was to meet Aaron, Darnell overslept. He jumped out of bed, rushed to the bathroom and met Lester coming out of the shower.

"What's up Darnell, no school today?" Lester asked.

"I'm late and I gotta take a leak," Darnell responded.

"So go ahead... leak," Lester grinned.

Darnell stood and pissed into the toilet while Lester stood naked and watched.

"Looks like that thing is all swole up on you boy," Lester teased.

"Don't temp me bitch or I'll stick it right up yo ass," Darnell replied. "You owe me some ass anyway."

Lester turned around bent over and spread his ass-cheeks, "Is this tempting enough for you?" he asked

"Damn...bitch!" Darnell replied shaking the last drops of piss off his rapidly hardening dick. Lester dropped to his knees and began sucking Darnell's young hard-on.

"Um...yeah...all right bitch. I'm gonna fuck that ass this time," Darnell cried out as he stepped from his pajamas. "You asked for it...shit...uh-huh. Yeah suck it Les baby."

Lester reached into the vanity and took out some baby oil. He poured oil on Darnell's hard young dick and poured some into the crack of his own ass, massaging the oil into his asshole with one hand while massaging Darnell's dick with the other. "All right daddy I'm gonna pay my debt. You been wanting this ass and now you are going to get it," Lester promised.

Darnell's heart began pounding wildly; he couldn't believe this was actually happening. He was really gonna put his dick in Lester's ass. All thoughts of Aaron had left his mind as Lester smoothly massaged his throbbing dick and balls.

"Let me put it in," Lester said.

"Sure baby sure," Darnell quickly agreed.

Lester stood up and bent over. He stretched out one arm to the sink and reached back with the other and grabbed Darnell's dick. "Take your hands and spread that ass open," he instructed. Darnell quickly complied and Lester guided the young boy's hard-on right into his

asshole. First just the head popped in and Lester moaned. He took a deep breath and as he exhaled he pushed backwards taking Darnell's dick about halfway up his tight ass. He put both hands on the sink, pulled forward slightly and pushed back again taking more dick. Again he pulled forward and pushed back.

Darnell was speechless but he caught on to the rhythm. He put his hands on Lester's shoulders and started pumping his dick in and out.

"Oh daddy fuck me...please daddy please..." Lester wailed.

"Oh hell yeah!" Darnell screamed out, thrilled as he looked down and watched his hard black dick sliding in and out of Lester's wide yellow ass.

"Do me good daddy, do me!" Lester pleaded. "Oooo...shit! Now let me hold it. Push it in as far as you can and don't move."

Darnell did as he was told. He had been smacking his hips against Lester's ass, now he plunged in deep and froze while Lester began using his ass muscles to quickly grip and release this dick he was enjoying so much. Darnell quickly caught on to this rhythm too and started deep grinding in Lester's ass.

"Oh shit daddy! Oh...no...no," Lester shouted while pumping his own semi-hard dick which was shooting cum onto the floor. He started grunting and slamming his ass into Darnell who enjoyed the most powerful climax of his young life. He dug his fingers into Lester's shoulders and went totally rigid as his dick exploded again and again and again. When he finally stopped shooting cum Darnell continued fucking Lester's ass. His cum had made it slick and juicy and it felt really good.

"Whew, shit you something else boy," Lester said.

"Yeah, told you bitch and I ain't through yet," Darnell bragged.

Lester straightened up causing Darnell's dick to slip from his ass. "Well come on then," he replied, "I gotta get more comfortable." He stepped away and marched straight to Darnell's bed where he lay on his back and brought his knees as close to his chest as he could get them. "You want some more man pussy boy, come and get it," he grinned.

Darnell responded instantly. He shoved his still hard dick into Lester's wet asshole and began pumping fast. Lester moaned with delight and somehow managed to turn over while keeping that dick in his ass. With his back to Darnell he humped his ass upwards giving the young man all he could handle.

"Come on daddy fuck baby Lester...oh yeah fuck me daddy...oh do it...do it!" Lester challenged.

"Ooo...you like dis dick in yo ass, don't you fag bitch?" Darnell grunted.

"Yes daddy...oh yes...yes...um...I love yo sweet black dick...fuck me! Fuck me...umm ummm," Lester moaned.

After only a very few minutes of furious fucking, Darnell again tensed then shot his cum into Lester's willing ass. He collapsed on top of Lester who loved every moment and wanted to keep Darnell's dick in his ass as long as possible. But in too short a time Darnell slid out and rolled off him. Lester quickly washed Darnell's dick then briefly sucked it but the young man was spent and drifting off into a sound peaceful sleep.

Darnell awoke to a noisy house. His sisters and his mother were home. On the table next to his bed was

an envelope with his name on it. It had been stuck under the front door and his sister put it on his table. Inside the envelope was a note that simply said, *"Thanks for nothing!" Aaron.* Darnell started to put his clothes on, but didn't feel like it. So he lay in bed and fondled his dick. He was thinking about having fucked Lester when Tamika knocked on his window. She could just reach it standing on the edge of the fire escape.

"Come down to the park so we can talk. Where's Aaron?" she questioned.

"Shit! I don't know where the fuck Aaron is! Come here!" Darnell ordered.

"Uh-uh. Jerk off and come on out," Tamika replied.

"Naw...come here Tamika!" Darnell pleaded. "Help me with this please. See how hard it is."

"That's your little problem Darnell!" Tamika advised. "Bring it to the park and maybe I'll help you with it. I've got to find Aaron."

Tamika disappeared and Darnell went back to stroking his dick. His mother called him to dinner and Darnell pumped furiously trying to cum. But to his amazement he couldn't, so he got dressed and went to dinner with a hard-on.

After eating Darnell went to the park. He spotted Tamika and Aaron leaning against the fence. "What's up?" he asked.

"Listen," Tamika responded, "we gotta chill on the car raids for a while. It ain't much fun anymore anyway and some people are getting suspicious."

"But I like doing cars!" Aaron protested.

"No, we gotta chill!" Tamika insisted.

"Yeah, that shit is dumb," Darnell agreed.

"Anyway we need to start doing shit for money," Tamika advised.

"Like what?" Aaron asked.

"Yeah what?" Darnell added.

"Let me worry about that!" Tamika replied. "It's gonna be big and we gonna make some money but I'm still working on it."

"You full of shit Tamika!" Aaron snorted.

Tamika stepped away shook her ass and said, "We'll see who is full of shit. Remember chill on the cars, later on dudes." She switched her ass across the park and disappeared into her apartment building.

Darnell patched things up with Aaron by promising to tell him everything about his morning with Lester. When he finished his story his dick was super hard and he was out of breath. But Aaron was not impressed.

"So you didn't suck his dick huh?" he asked.

"Well no, but I don't want to suck Lester's dick," Darnell replied.

"Do you want to suck mine?" Aaron questioned.

"What?" Darnell asked.

"You heard me. Do you want to suck my dick or not? I'll suck yours if you suck mine," Aaron pleaded.

"You'll suck mine even if I don't suck yours, won't you?" Darnell challenged.

"Well...yeah." Aaron admitted. "But you said you would do me too."

"Okay..." Darnell agreed, "but where?"

"Let's go around back," Aaron suggested.

They searched for nearly half an hour but privacy could not be found that evening, so they stood behind a car, jacked each other off then went home.

The next day the two boys left school early, went to Aaron's house and immediately undressed. Darnell was of average height, slim, with delicate features and smooth dark skin. Aaron was short, kinda chunky and real light-skinned. It was the first time they had seen each other completely naked and Darnell was amazed at how big Aaron's dick really was. It was at least eight inches long and real thick with a heavy foreskin. They were quite a contrast lying on the floor each stroking the other.

Aaron made the first move. He leaned over and sucked Darnell's dick into his mouth. He wanted it, he loved it and he sucked with great enthusiasm.

Darnell loved it too. He watched Aaron suck him for a few moments then closely inspected Aaron's big hard dick in his hand and pulled the foreskin back and forth. Slowly Darnell brought Aaron's dick to his mouth. First he kissed it, then he licked it and after he decided he liked the taste and feel of it, Darnell slid the dick into his mouth. Aaron squealed with delight, but Darnell was in another world, way beyond anything he had known until now. The dick in his mouth was causing jolts of excitement to soar through his body and he couldn't get enough. Like Aaron, he seemed to take to this new activity naturally. He gagged repeatedly trying to suck all of it and didn't back off when Aaron came in his throat.

They sucked each other off twice more that day. Then a couple days later Darnell got his dick into Aaron's ass. It took a lot of grunting and sweating but he got it in then fucked Aaron hard and fast. Aaron loved it and he was in love. He wanted Darnell to be his boyfriend but Darnell was starting to think of himself as

a stud and of Aaron as a pet bitch.

When Darnell bragged to Tamika about first sucking then fucking Aaron she was disappointed. She had wanted to watch the action and see Darnell get his ass fucked not the other way around. When she questioned Darnell about him sucking Aaron she made note of the fact that he was casual about his response, and did not think sucking a dick was a real big deal. So she introduced Darnell to a small time dope dealer called TJ, then shocked Darnell by ordering him to suck TJ in front of her for a few joints. TJ was game and because Tamika ordered him to, Darnell obeyed then started regularly sucking TJ for dope.

For reasons known only to him, Darnell went out of his way to pursue then fuck a handicapped girl named Lisa. He knew her fourteen-year old brother was watching them and the next day Darnell caught the boy on his way to school. He pushed him behind some bushes, snatched his pants down then sucked his dick. Quietly Darnell was amazed. This young boy's dick was bigger than his and jumped hard the instant his mouth made contact. Delighted the young boy pulled Darnell's hair and rapidly fucked his mouth. Suddenly he trembled and cried-out as Darnell tasted a small amount of pubescent cum. Then for a few moments the young boy moaned and slowly slid his dick in and out of Darnell's mouth before yanking up his pants and running away.

Darnell went home and found Lester still sleeping. He slowly slid the sheet down and was delighted to find Lester nude and semi-hard. He undressed then leaned over and sucked Lester's entire dick into his mouth then held it perfectly still. He could

feel Lester's dick getting harder and bigger inside his mouth and was freaking with the feeling. Lester began grinding his hips and grunting as he awakened, causing Darnell to swing one leg over him and drop his dick into Lester's mouth. On this morning Lester awoke in ecstasy. He eagerly sucked Darnell's dick while Darnell sucked his. Lester was beyond thrilled, never had he awaken like this before. He moaned with delight as the two of them nosily slurped and sucked each other to climax.

Darnell should have been full of himself. He fucked ass and chased pussy. He sucked dicks and got his own dick sucked. But despite all this fucking around Darnell was confused, obsessed and far from being at sexual peace with himself. Now that he got a chance to actually fuck, he still came to damn fast and somehow cumming just wasn't enough. Darnell's own dick was a disappointment to him and he wasn't ready to admit to himself that of all his sexual experiences his biggest thrills so far came from sucking dicks. He really loved sucking Aaron's big dick but made Aaron think it was no big deal. He also fucked Aaron and Lester when he got the chance but made it clear to them his ass was off limits. Yet in spite of that, Darnell really wanted to get fucked. He badly wanted to know what it would feel like but he didn't want just any dick. Deep inside he knew he only wanted Drey to fuck him. He didn't understand why and wasn't really sure he could go through with it. He was scared to death to admit it, even to Tamika or LaKeisha, although they seemed to bring it up a lot. He wanted to fuck Tamika in her butt but she wouldn't let him. In fact Tamika wouldn't let him fuck her at all and LaKeisha always demanded a high price.

Her latest offering was to let Darnell fuck her if he let Drey fuck him in his ass at the same time and she again confronted him.

"I don't know..." Darnell hedged.

"Aw shit grow up boy!" LaKeisha demanded. "You know you want Drey's meat up your ass and he wants to give it to you, so what's the problem huh?"

"I don't know Keish, your brother might hurt me," Darnell whimpered. "I ain't no fag! I ain't never had a dick in my booty."

"You said you want to fuck and get fucked at the same time didn't you?" LaKeisha demanded. "Well? You DID say that didn't you?"

"Yeah I said it...so what?" Darnell responded.

"Well then there's only one way to do that!" LaKeisha snapped. "Fuck me and let Drey fuck you, right...? Huh...? Well...what's up? You game or not?" she questioned.

"I don't know, shit...I gotta think about this," Darnell whined.

"Aw fuck you Darnell! Call me when you grow up boy!" LaKeisha snorted.

"Naw...really...I gotta think about this," Darnell pleaded.

"Come on Tamika let's go," LaKeisha responded.

The two girls left and Darnell agonized. *Sucking a dick was not a real big thing but getting fucked in his butt was totally different. Everybody would know and he would be branded a fag.* He thought about Drey's dick, he had heard it was real big. *Would it hurt? Would he like it? Why Drey? Why did he only want Drey to fuck him? He didn't really even know Drey. Why does his asshole tingle and spasm when he thinks about Drey fucking him? In fact* Darnell

wondered, *why couldn't he even look at Drey without feeling weak, and why could he absolutely not look into Drey's eyes.*

His thoughts were interrupted by his neighbor...a plain skinny middle-aged woman. She was offering him a couple of dollars to carry some packages from her car up to her apartment. Darnell agreed and lugged the packages up the stairs. When he got them all in, the lady paid him and asked if he wanted to rest a minute. He looked into her eyes and instinctively knew he could fuck her. He reached out and began unbuttoning her blouse. She made no move to stop him and when her panties hit the floor, she returned the favor and undressed him. Darnell pulled her close and softly kissed her while she ran her fingers over his chest and shoulders. He squeezed her ass and kissed her softly on the neck. The lady gasped and shuddered while her hands traveled down Darnell's stomach and quickly on to stroke and massage his young hard-on against her clit. After several moments, she lay back on her couch and Darnell eased down on top of her. He was quite amazed that his dick located the pussy and slipped right in on the first try and without any real help. The lady smelled good and her soft wet pussy was hot and inviting. She wrapped her legs around Darnell's back and pumped her ass up to meet his every stroke, but Darnell couldn't take it. With one final stroke he came and then collapsed. He hated himself for cumming so soon and was embarrassed.

"I... I'm sorry," he stammered.

"Don't be," she replied. "I enjoyed it."

"Next time will be better," he offered.

"I'm sure it will be sweetie, what's your name?" she asked.

"Uh, Darnell."

"I'm Kay, Darnell…and just so you know, I'm a quicker hitter too, so I really did enjoy it. Now…would you like to clean up, relax a spell, maybe have a drink or something," she offered.

"Naw no thanks, I gotta go." Darnell mumbled as he struggled into his clothes and headed for the front door.

"You know where to find me Darnell sweetie," Kay called after him. "Will I see you again?"

"Yeah…sure!" Darnell promised. "Bye Kay and thanks you was great."

"You were too sweetie," Kay responded.

Darnell headed for home, his head now more fucked up than ever.

Chapter five

About an hour before sunrise, Tamika awoke in a fit of terror. Her dream that night was her absolute worst nightmare. Sweating, breathing hard and scared to death she leapt out of bed and ran to her mother's room. "Mama! Mama!" she cried, violently shaking Ruth Ann.

"Huh, whut…whut?" Ruth Ann whined.

"Mama wake up!" Tamika demanded.

Ruth Ann rolled over and opened her eyes. The terror she saw in her daughter's face startled her. She sat up and reached out for Tamika's hand. "Whut's da matter baby? Huh? Sit down heah and tell me bout it," she instructed.

"Mama is Uncle Wint my daddy?" Tamika fearfully asked.

"Whut? Unka who?" Ruth Ann demanded.

"Uncle Wint is he my daddy?" Tamika repeated. "Is he?"

"Tamika whut da hell you takin bout?" Ruth Ann questioned. "Whut's wrong wit you gurl? And who dis Unka Wint?"

"You know Uncle Wint!" Tamika insisted. "He lives in this building and he fixes cars round back...and I had this dream that he was my daddy, and..."

"Wint? You means Winston Littles?" Ruth Ann asked.

"Yeah, yeah Winston Littles!" Tamika confirmed.

"Lemme get dis shit straight. You askin me if Winston Littles is yo daddy?" Ruth Ann quizzed. "Is dat whut you askin me?"

"Yeah...is he?" Tamika asked again.

"Paww...ha-ha-haaaa-ha-ha-ha...sheeit Tamika! Carry yo ass back tuh bed gurl...ha-ha-ha...Winston Littles ain't nobodies daddy! Ha-ha-ha...he ain't yo uncle either hee-hee...sheeit," Ruth Ann cackled.

"Tell me about him," Tamika pleaded.

"Ah ain't tellin you shit, cept take yo ass back tuh bed and stay way from old Winston Littles!"

"But you used to like him didn't you?" Tamika prodded.

"Tamika! Gurl...you better take yo ass back ta bed and quit fuckin wit me. Winston Littles ain't nuthin but an old dog...yo daddy sheeit...hee-hee-hee." Ruth Ann drifted off and within a few moments was again sound asleep.

Tamika went back to bed but didn't sleep. She sat up thinking. When morning came she left for school early, going instead to Darnell's apartment. She banged on his bedroom window until Darnell stuck his head out.

"What's up?" he asked.

"Go over to TJ's and get me about five joints," Tamika ordered.

"When?"

"Now!"

"This early?" Darnell questioned.

"What did I just say?" Tamika snapped.

"TJ gonna be pissed off if I wake him up!" Darnell pleaded.

"You can handle that, now quit stalling!"

"I ain't got no money Tamika!" Darnell whined.

"Don't even try it Darnell!" Tamika shot back. "You ain't never paid TJ with money, all you need is your mouth and you know it, so stop fucking around. I'll be waiting in the park, hurry up this is important."

Darnell grumbled but as always he did whatever Tamika told him to do. He went to TJ's apartment and was surprised to find TJ happy to see him. He liked TJ's dope, but he didn't really like sucking him for it. TJ would grab Darnell's ears and fuck his mouth real fast, pushing deep into his throat making Darnell gag and whimper. This morning was no different, in short order TJ was delighted and Darnell got what he came for. He found Tamika in the park and gave her an envelope containing five freshly rolled joints. "You going to school or what?" he asked.

"Naw, I told you I got some important shit to do today, catch you later," Tamika replied then headed for Wanda's apartment.

Wanda was Ruth Ann's best friend but they were more like sisters than friends. Their relationship ran hot and cold but they had more or less hung together since high school. Wanda was the older of the two and a lot more mellow. A few years back Tamika caught Wanda fucking her brother Sam. Using Nuggy as a shield Tamika had stolen some candy from Wilson's Variety Store and to avoid sharing she ran home to eat it then

hid behind the living room drapes when Sam and Wanda came through the door.

"Git dem clothes off young mutherfucker," Wanda demanded. "You been talkin shit long enough now we gonna throw down for real! Git em off, hurry up!"

Within minutes they were fucking up a storm and Tamika watched with wide excited eyes. She was thrilled with the show and had no intention of making her presence known but a sudden sneeze gave her away. Both Sam and Wanda promised her favors and begged her to keep quiet which she did. Everyone knew Sam was Ruth Ann's favorite child and at the very least she would literally cut Wanda's titties off for fucking her baby. Tamika was confident as she knocked on the door. Wanda owed her and she had plenty of good weed to loosen her up.

Groggy and grumpy Wanda opened the door. "Tamika! Gurl...what you want this early?" she demanded.

"I need to talk to you," Tamika advised.

"Sheeit, gurlfriend I don't feel like no talkin right now. I'm gettin ready to kill Pookey's ass if he don't get the fuck out of heah and go to school!" Wanda fumed. "POOKEY! POOKEY? Yo ass better not be back in dat bed! Ain't yo ass supposed to be movin toward school too Miss Tamika?"

"I told you I need to talk and I got some killer smoke," Tamika responded.

"Lemme see?" Wanda demanded.

Tamika handed Wanda a joint, which she promptly lit. "Hum...this shit got a good taste...uh huh, sho do," she observed. "Take yo ass on out in the kitchen

and make me some coffee Miss Thang, then we'll talk a minute. POOKEY! Goddamnit I'm gonna kill yo ass boy!"

After a few minutes, Pookey hurried toward the front door. "Chill out sugar booty!" he called to Wanda.

"Boy, git yo ass to school," Wanda growled.

Pookey blew her a kiss then disappeared out the door.

Wanda stubbed out the joint, put it into her stash box then went to the kitchen. Tamika was sitting at the table with two steaming cups of coffee and two big joints waiting. Wanda sat down with a sigh. She sipped the coffee, lit one of the joints, took a deep drag, held it then exhaled. "Dis really is some good shit, were you get it?"

"TJ."

"TJ?" Wanda asked in surprise. "TJ back on the street?"

"Yeah! He been back."

"Shaddup! I didn't know that...TJ always did have good shit. I gots to check him out...uh huh...sho do! He living over there with his mama?" Wanda asked.

"Uh-huh," Tamika responded.

"Good, real good...sheeit you done brung me some good news gurlfriend...uh huh...some real good news...ha-ha," Wanda chuckled. "Now...Miss Tamika Rochelle what's dis shit you wanna talk about...huh?"

"Don't call me Rochelle!" Tamika pleaded.

"I like that name...I nicknamed you Chelley, member?" Wanda reminisced.

"Aw...Auntie Wanny," Tamika replied.

"Okay! Okay...truce gurlfriend, you knows I can't stand dat Auntie Wanny shit," Wanda declared. "Now what you wanna talk about... huh?"

"Uncle Wint!" Tamika announced.

"Who?" Wanda responded.

"Uncle Wint...Winston Littles," Tamika replied.

"Winston Littles! My, my, my, what in the world you want to know about Winston?" Wanda asked.

"Is he my daddy?" Tamika questioned.

"WHAT? Ah-ha-ha-ha-ha-haaa...whew...sheeit! Naw baby gurl, he damn sho ain't yo daddy! Ha-ha-ha-ha...ah ha-ha-ha...whew, where the hell you get that idea? Ha-ha-ha-ha," Wanda continued to laugh.

"Why's that so funny?" Tamika demanded.

"Lord child if you only knew...ha-ha-ha."

"Tell me...please?" Tamika pleaded.

"What you reaching for?" Wanda suddenly questioned.

"The joint," Tamika replied.

"You got one don't you?" Wanda inquired.

"Yeah."

"Well you smoke it, dis ones mines!" Wanda instructed.

"Tell me about Uncle Wint," Tamika pleaded again.

"What about him huh?" Wanda chuckled. "He just an old dog."

"That's what mama said, but she used to go with him didn't she?" Tamika asked.

"Gurlfriend all dat shit went down way before you was even born, whut you wanna know about all dat for?" Wanda inquired.

"Okay, deal. You tell me all about Uncle Wint, then I'll tell you why I want to know," Tamika offered.

"Naw, bullshit, here the deal! If you don't tell me why you wants to know, I ain't gonna tell you shit Miss

Thang," Wanda corrected.

"Okay…okay!" Tamika agreed, "Last night I dreamed Uncle Wint was really my daddy and I got to know, I mean…I just gotta know that ain't possible!"

"Why baby?" Wanda asked. "Why you so worried about that?"

"Cause I just gotta know Wanda…I just gotta know!" Tamika insisted.

"Tamika! What's da real reason you gots to know?" Wanda demanded.

"Cause…cause I plan to marry him, that's why!" Tamika confessed.

"What??? Lordy Tamika, you ain't been makin truck wid dat man have you?" Wanda asked in astonishment.

"Ha! I wish!" Tamika snorted. "But that doesn't mean I'm not going to."

"Does Winston know bout yo big plan?" Wanda asked.

"He don't take me serious, but he will, you'll see. Now tell me about him and you and mama," Tamika pleaded.

Wanda chuckled, "Get me duh bourbon outta dat cabinet dere," she instructed. After topping off her coffee she leaned back in her chair. "I member when Winston first moved in here. Nelson Park was a lot nicer then and he was about the only young single man dat had his own apartment. He got in cause he was on disability from the service, though I ain't never seen nothing disabled about him. He sho was fine back then and had a real flashy car. Gurl ole Winston was all the rage. Just about every old cow in these projects was trying to give him some…uh huh…sho was! I didn't pay him no mind

though cause I was living with Big Chester. You didn't know Chester but he was a real jealous man and violent! Gurl let me tell you Chester didn't need no reason. If he just thought I was fucking around all hell would break loose and stay loose way too damn long. But enyhow not long after Winston moved in here, Big Chester got in trouble with the law for whupping some old white man. I went downtown and bailed him out of jail and Chester's fool ass went straight to the hospital, dragged that same old white man right outta his hospital bed then whupped his old behind again. Chester messed that old man up real bad before they stopped him and the police got up there. They tried Big Chester for attempted murder and gave him thirty-six years honey. Thirty-six years to life, he ain't never gonna get out."

Wanda paused, taking a long deep drag from her joint followed by a long drink of spiked coffee. "Well after that I started hanging with Ruth Ann a lot more but all she could talk about was Winston Littles. Winston this, Winston that I was sick of hearing about Winston. Half the wenches in Nelson Park was trying to get pregnant by Winston and yo mama's ass was leading the parade."

"Get pregnant?" Tamika questioned.

"Damn right! Shit if you had Winston's baby you had it going on gurlfriend," Wanda advised.

"Why?"

"Why? Sheeit!" Wanda chuckled. "First you would get more welfare AND you'd have Winston's fine ass right where you wanted it. Winston was a hustler honey. He had his own place, a nice car, he was getting disability money, he fixed cars and at that time he was dealing weed too. Shit you'd be queen bee with

Winston's baby in yo belly. I still wasn't interested in him though till one day he came up here trying to get me to sell him Big Chester's old car. Big Chester had been gone about ten months and to tell you the truth…in all that time, I hadn't even thought about having no sex or nothing. I don't know I guess I just figured there wasn't no more Big Chesters and I could rub my ole thang and make it feel good without it being sore. So I don't know…I just wasn't thinking bout no sex. But I guess I musta been getting kinda lonesome, you know what I mean gurlfriend? Shit before I knew what time it was ole Winston had me in his arms and ready to go. Now let me tell you something Tamika. Before that day I thought sex wasn't supposed to last more than a couple minutes and if a man's thang wasn't big enough to make you sore, he wasn't shit! Ha ha…sound funny now but back den I believed dat shit cause dat's what I was tole…and you know a lot of dese women ain't never learnt no damn different…ha-ha-ha. Gurlfriend I mean I used to make it my business to see a man's thang before he got anything heah. Uh huh…sho did…and baby-gurl if he wasn't hung like a donkey, he didn't get none of this! Oh no! Now don't get me wrong child, Winston ain't no little man in dat department but Chester wasn't called BIG because of his feet. Ha-ha-ha…gurl Chester had the biggest thang I ever seen and he didn't fuck round wit you neither. He'd throw me down and in just a couple of minutes make me sore as hell. It never did take him long and you know something…he never once got more than half of his big ole thang inside me and I wanted all of it sooo bad. He would hit it a few strokes den cum real hard and just fall right on top of me and go to sleep. I'd push his big ass off me and lay there next to

him and rub my sore thang wit his cum. Shit da rubbing was da best part. Ha-ha-ha…it was."

Tamika refilled Wanda's cup, half bourbon and half coffee.

Wanda took a long drink and continued. "But Winston, Lord, gurl Winston was so SMOOTH. That man got me so goddamn hot I couldn't stand it! Do you hear me? We was talking about Big Chester's old car when he put on a record and got me to slow dancing you know? He started rubbing my back, kissing my neck, nibbling and whispering sweet shit in my ear. Gurlfriend…sheeit…ha-ha! I just turned into a puddle of jelly and melted all over his fine ass. Something about Winston was just different you know. He was all man but patient and gentle. He completely undressed me in my living room then picked me up and carried me to my bed and started kissing me all over. Now Tamika you gotta understand that back in them days, black men didn't eat no pussy, not like they do now, and even if they was…hadn't nobody ate mine. But gurl…let me tell you! When Winston's tongue started whuppin da man on da mountain, I screamed so loud and long I knows dey heard me all way over in da park! It's a wunder I didn't pull dat man's hair out. Sheeit…I'm getting myself all worked up just thinking about that day. Winston just knew what to do. Gurlfriend…sheeit…let me tell you! The man took his time, he had me way past ready when he pinned my legs back against my shoulders. Uumph…started sucking my lips and kissing me with real wet kisses, slid his thang into me and babychild he worked dis pussy dat day…uh huh…he sho did." Wanda was rocking back and forth as she talked. "Just between you and me Tamika, Winston Littles taught me

what da fuck sex was all about dat day and I wouldn't lie about that. Shit...Winston Littles didn't just fuck...naw...oh no! Winston Littles made love honey! I mean, I just kept getting off and it was feeling sooo good...sheeit. I ain't thought about dat in years but I ain't never gonna forget it. Winston's fine ass was so good...I hadn't never got down that long and loved every second of it like that. Ha-ha-ha...I gave Winston Big Chester's old car. Ha-ha-ha...ha-ha-ha-ah-ha-ha-ha...I sho did! Wasn't nothing Big Chester could do for me after Winston...and I do mean nothing! Hell he was locked up anyway. Ha-ha-ha...still is. Well, well...let me see...truth is, after that day I became just one more wench trying to have Winston's baby. But shit da man was just plain good honey. And living in here he got a lot of opportunities and didn't pass up many either. Now I wasn't gonna out and out chase him like Ruth Ann did, so I didn't get many chances at him, but I sho made the most of it when I did...ha-ha-ha. Uh huh...sho did. I told Ruth Ann about it and that fool went completely off on me. I thought I was gonna have to kill her crazy ass. After that she hardly spoke to me for nearly a year, then one day she come flying through my front door crying, screaming and waving this paper all around. She swore she was going to cut off Winston's thang and shove it up his ass. Ha-ha-ha...hadn't been for me she'd ah done it too, ha-ha-ha," Wanda laughed loudly.

"WHY? Why she wanna do that?" Tamika asked in horror.

"Turns out she'd been prying through Winston's personal shit and found this Army paper," Wanda explained. "I didn't understand most of it, it was some

kind of medical shit, but it said Winston had a VASECTOMY! Ha-ha-ha…ah-ha-ha-ha-ha. Here ole Winston with his fine ass, been humpin nearly every wench in Nelson Park and shootin nothing but BLANKS…ha-ha-ha…all these wenches trying to have his baby…me and Ruth Ann included…ha-ha-haa…and ole Winston was having the time of his life…shootin blanks all over the projects. Ha-ha-ha…ahh…ha-ha-haa…whew! It wasn't funny then tho…ha-ha-ha…oh my. I calmed Ruth Ann down some but she went straight to the park and loud talked Winston in front of everybody. She been mad at him ever since. Lot of these wenches still mad at Winston…ha-ha-ha hee-hee. Most of them cut his ass completely off too…ha-ha-ha-ha. Ruth Ann cut him way back but she didn't cut him completely off. Finally he just stopped messing with her at all. Though I'll bet she wouldn't refuse him now if he hit on her for some, shit…neither would I for that matter. Now you got yo big eyes trained on him huh?"

"I'm gonna marry him!" Tamika declared.

"You!" Wanda chuckled. "Tamika I hate to tell you this gurlfriend but you ain't got no chance at that. I ain't never knowed Winston to mess with no jail bait…ha-ha-ha."

"I'll be eighteen in just a few months and I'm gonna marry him! You'll see!" Tamika insisted.

"Yeah…uh huh…you right Miss Thang I'll believe that when I see it," Wanda advised still chuckling.

"Did he ever get married?" Tamika asked.

"Naw…not that I know anything about," Wanda replied.

"Well thanks Wanda, at least I know for sure he ain't my daddy," Tamika sighed "I'm really glad he ain't

but I'm kinda sad too."

"Why you sad?" Wanda questioned.

"I don't know…I guess…it's just…I don't know…I guess I just ain't never gonna know who my daddy really is," Tamika responded.

"I know who yo daddy is," Wanda advised.

"You do? Who? Who is he Wanda? Who? WHO?" Tamika demanded.

"Now you listen heah Tamika, I been talking to you cause I owe you. I ain't forgot, I knows I owe you, but after I tell you this, you be gone Miss Thang…and we even…heah? I'm tellin you shit ah ain't never told nobody and I don't owe you shit no mo, you hear me Tamika Martin? And anuther thing, you ain't heard none of dis shit from me…unnerstand?" Wanda demanded.

"Yeah! Who's my daddy?" Tamika pleaded.

"His name was Benny!" Wanda announced.

"Benny! Benny who?" Tamika shrieked.

"Shit, I don't know. He used to work at the Playmore Lounge. Me and Ruth Ann used to hang in there. Benny called himself a singer but most of the time he was the bartender," Wanda advised.

"Where's he now?" Tamika questioned.

"I'm sorry baby, but Benny got took out years ago, something to do with drugs I think," Wanda replied.

"How you know he's my daddy?" Tamika questioned.

"Tell you what you do Miss Thang!" Wanda snapped. "You march yo smart ass down to the Playmore and see for yo self. There's a lot of pictures on the wall behind the bar and Benny's up there too. Hell you can't miss him…you look just like him. Uh huh

JUST like him." Wanda stood up and looked out the window down into the courtyard. "There's ole DW! Dancing Willie...look at em, with his fine brown ass, sho would like some of that right now...uh huh...sho would."

"I gotta go Wanda," Tamika announced.

"Yeah, sho gurlfriend," Wanda replied. "HEY! Member you ain't heard none of dis shit from me. Fact is, I ain't even seen yo ass lately...now bye. Go on Willie...dance baby...uh huh!"

Tamika laid another joint on the table. "Thanks Wanda I'm gonna do something nice for you...bye now," she called out.

"Yeah...uh huh...uh huh...bye Miss Thang," Wanda replied.

Tamika ran down the steps. She had never been so happy or excited. She raced across the courtyard stopping only to talk to Dancing Willie. After their short conversation they slapped five and Willie was grinning. He spun around and started moon walking toward the entrance to Wanda's building. Tamika headed straight to the Playmore Lounge.

Chapter six

It was 9:51 a.m. when Tamika started beating on the glass doors of the Playmore Lounge.

At 10:05 a.m. an old man named Phil opened the door. He rubbed his head, blinked his runny bloodshot eyes, squinted into the sun then focused on Tamika. "Whys youse raisin awl dis ruckus gal? Dis jaint ain't opin, doan opin till foe," he declared.

"I want to see my daddy's picture!" Tamika responded.

"Whut? Yo daddies pickure?" Phil questioned.

"Yeah, his name is Benny and his picture is on the wall behind the bar," Tamika replied.

"Ah doan knows nuthin bout no pickures, ah cleans up round heah...youns can't git in heah nohow till foe clock. Cum back den huneychile and sees Mistuh Rudolph...annudder thang...you sho is ah purty little gal...damn shame ah cants call back a few yeahs! Sheeit...a'd be's on youse liks quik on silver!" Phil responded with a grin, exposing his two remaining but badly yellowed teeth.

"Oooo...you sexy ole dog...four o'clock huh? I'll

be here, thanks…bye now," Tamika responded.

"Ay huneychile…ay…young as youse looks tuh be, u'd bettah gos tuh da back doe, if'n youse cums back nah," Phil advised.

"Okay I will, thanks…SugarPaw," Tamika replied.

At 3:26 p.m. Tamika started pounding on the back door of the Playmore Lounge.

At 3:29 p.m. Geno could stand it no longer. "Somebody answer that damn door," Geno demanded. "Rudy? RUDY! PHILLIP! GEORGETTE? TONI? Well where the hell is everybody? Aw…I guess can't nobody hear that door but me…huh? Somebody answer that damn door before I go off back here…RUUDDY! RUDY! Well shit…okay…alright I'll answer it my damn self."

Geno was a female impersonator; who was applying make-up and getting ready for another performance, another night at the Playmore. Now fully agitated he marched out of his dressing room half dressed, half made up and flung open the back door.

Startled, Tamika jumped back but when she saw Geno she started giggling.

Geno looked at her and in spite of himself he started giggling too. "What you want chile bean?" Geno asked between giggles. "Aw come on in here, I don't know what you want but it sure must be important with you making all that damn noise."

"Why you dressed like that?" Tamika asked still giggling.

"Why am I dressed like this? What's your name?" Geno demanded.

"Tamika Martin."

"Well Miss Tamika Martin in the first place I'm only half dressed, not that much, and in the second place

did you see that poster out front for the Divine Miss Gina Devine? Did you see it?" Geno questioned.

"Yeah I saw it," Tamika admitted.

"Well honey...I'm the Divine Miss Gina Devine!" Geno proudly announced.

"What?" Tamika asked in disbelief.

"Well right now I kinda half Gina Devine and half Eugene Watson and...oh look at the time. Come on, you wanna watch me make up before Rudy throws your young ass outta here."

"Yeah," a wide-eyed Tamika replied then followed Geno to his dressing room. "Who's Rudy?" she asked.

"He claims to own the place but really he's just the manager," Gino stated matter-of-factly.

Tamika closely watched Geno transform into a woman, almost forgetting why she was there. "Why you wanna be a woman?" she asked.

"I don't want to be a woman I just dress up like one and entertain folks," Geno chuckled.

"You like men?" Tamika inquired.

"Well... let's put it this way chile bean I got four children and two ex-wives," Geno replied with a big grin. "This is a job. A good paying job, though I got a little freak in me too. I just love being the Divine Miss Gina Devine."

"Why?" Tamika questioned.

"Why? Why? Worship...honey...WOR...SHIP!" Geno declared. "They worship Miss Gina Devine's ass and I eat that shit up! But hold on here and let me ask you a question," he continued. "What you come here for...beating on that door all that time?"

"I came to see my daddy's picture," Tamika

responded. "His name is Benny and his picture is on a wall behind the bar and I ain't never seen him or nothing and..."

"Well I'll be double damn damned...Benny Monroe! I knew there was something too familiar about you. Ump, ump, ump! Chile bean ain't no denying it! You is damn sure Benny Monroe's child...got that same ole gap between your front teeth...ha-ha," Geno chuckled.

"Let me see him...did you know him?" Tamika pleaded, then questioned.

"Yeah I knew him, come on. Rudy! Hey Rudy look here this is Benny Monroe's little chile bean," Geno proudly announced.

"So what!" Rudy snapped.

"So what? This chile bean ain't never even seen what her daddy looks like she come to see his picture," Geno advised.

"Fuck Benny Monroe! He checked out owing me big. She can have his goddamn picture for all I care. AND...get her ass outta here before four o'clock Geno! What's yo mama's name girl?" Rudy demanded.

"Tamika...I mean Ruth Ann Martin."

"GENO!" Rudy shouted.

"I know, I know!" Geno replied. "Here chile bean, you heard the man you can have the picture. A word of warning though, if you show that picture to Ruth Ann she gonna tear it up, you got that?"

Tamika stared at the picture, lightly running her fingers over Benny's face, "Yeah...thanks! I mean thanks a lot!" she beamed.

"You welcome a lot, now get on home!" Geno smiled. "Wait! Wait a minute...wait a minute...take a

picture of the Divine Miss Gina Devine too. Here I'll autograph it for you, gimme a pen...gimme a pen. Rudy gimme your pen," Geno demanded.

"Goddamnit Geno!" Rudy growled.

"Gimme the pen! What was your name again chile bean?" Geno asked with a happy grin.

"Tamika."

"Yeah, that's right...okay. *To my real good friend Tamika - have a great life - Gina Devine*, there! Here chile bean now scoot," Geno proudly concluded.

Tamika ran all the way back to Nelson Park. "Look Uncle Wint! Look. LOOK!" she shouted. She was beaming, eyes shining and nearly out of breath. "I got a picture of my daddy. His name is Benny Monroe and he was a singer at the Playmore Lounge and...LOOK!"

"Let me see that," I responded and took a close look at the picture. "Uh huh...I remember this cat, heard him sing a few times."

"Everybody says I look just like him," Tamika bragged.

"Well tell you what baby, ain't no doubt he yo daddy all right, but you a whole lot better looking than he ever was," I assured.

"Oooo Uncle Wint, I love you. Was my daddy a good singer?" Tamika asked.

"Yeah he was pretty good really, done a lot of Marvin Gaye's stuff, kinda sounded like Marvin a little too," I honestly replied.

"Did you know him?" Tamika questioned.

"Naw I never actually met the brother I just heard him sing a few times," I responded.

"I'm so happy I know who my Daddy is and I got his picture," Tamika beamed.

"Well I'm happy for you," I replied.

"Hug me Uncle Wint!" Tamika pleaded. "Oooo shit I ain't never gonna let you go."

"Quit damnit, you got your hug now go on," I responded.

"I'm going...I'm going...but not for long Uncle Wint," Tamika promised.

"Yeah, where have I heard that before?" I mumbled.

"I mean it Uncle Wint you'll see...you mine!" Tamika insisted with a knowing smile.

In short order she rounded up her cousin LaKeisha and her two brothers, Sam and Nuggy. After each had examined Benny Monroe's picture they all agreed. They knew Sam and Nuggy's father and neither LaKeisha nor either of Tamika's sisters looked anything like Benny Monroe so he was Tamika's father only. Satisfied she had Benny all to herself Tamika took his picture home and carefully hid it.

By seven o'clock that same evening, Darnell Freeman found himself the unwilling victim of Tamika and LaKeisha's efforts to turn him into a woman. Tamika had shown LaKeisha Geno's picture then told her all about him and her visit to the Playmore Lounge. The two of them were sure they could make Darnell look even better than Geno.

"Hold still damnit!" LaKeisha snapped, she was trying to apply make-up to Darnell's face. "How am I gonna get this shit right with you jerking around?"

"Hey! I don't remember saying I wanted to do this shit anyway!" Darnell complained.

"Shut-up Darnell!" Tamika demanded. She was stuffing a bra with socks. "You want your little ole thang

played with don't you?"

"Hell yeah!" Darnell replied.

"Well shut-up and be still!"

"This hair...I can't hide this shit, you need to shave Darnell!" LaKeisha demanded.

"No way...forget that, I ain't shaving nothing!" Darnell insisted.

"Take off your shirt," Tamika ordered.

"Watch out damnit! I told you he should dress before I put his make-up on!" LaKeisha shrieked.

"Okay," Tamika agreed. She ordered Darnell out of his clothes then into the bra and a tight short dress that belonged to Ruth Ann. Ignoring Darnell's meager protests; LaKeisha finished his make-up then put one of Ruth Ann's best wigs on his head.

Finally the two girls stepped back to appraise their work before allowing Darnell to see himself in Ruth Ann's full-length mirror. Darnell was absolutely stunned and could not believe what he was seeing. He wasn't just a guy in girl's clothes he WAS a girl! A gorgeous sexy fine bitch.

"He got long eyelashes naturally and that's good...but that hair on his face gotta go," LaKeisha insisted.

"Yeah, and you can see his thing sticking out but that's cool for now, we'll fix that shit tomorrow. Then we'll go for a walk pass the basketball courts on Larkspur Street," Tamika suggested.

"Good idea cuz," LaKeisha chimed.

"Naw it ain't! I...I don't know bout that!" Darnell stammered.

"Shut-up!" LaKeisha growled. "We wasn't asking, we was telling yo ass! Now let's take that shit off so you

can go home and shave...shave everything too!"

"But...I..." Darnell began.

"Shut-up!" Both girls demanded in unison.

Late that night Darnell lay in bed wide-awake. He was excited and without regret or hesitation had shaved his faint facial hair. *Damn!* He thought. *I really looked good. I'll bet I could be the finest bitch in Nelson Park...if I wanted to.* Something Darnell did not understand was stirring deep inside him. He grinned into the darkness and stroked his hard-on before finally falling asleep.

Chapter seven

Despite the fact Darnell had smooth skin and very little hair on his body, the next day Tamika and LaKeisha were armed with an electric razor and finished the job Darnell had only started. They shaved his arms, armpits, and any hair they could find on his chest, stomach, and legs. Then after a minor argument the three of them shaved Darnell's genitals.

With that done, they dressed him. First came Nuggy's jock strap. Nuggy was shorter than Darnell, so Tamika had rightly decided the smaller jock would better conceal his manhood. Then came two pair of LaKeisha's thickest panties, followed by a pair of cut off girls shorts, a tight-fitting stuffed bra, a sleeveless blouse, white ankle socks and Ruth Ann's low cut white sneakers. LaKeisha applied his make-up and used bobby pins to secure a short curly black wig. Tamika done his nails then put earrings and a necklace on him.

When the job was completed Darnell stepped before the mirror and was truly impressed. He studied his crotch and was very pleased. There was no hint of his male organ and the tight-fitting shorts made his ass

really stick out, round, firm and bouncy. Darnell was getting aroused just looking at himself and wanted to fuck his own ass. He felt a groundswell of confidence and knew he was a better-looking girl than either Tamika or LaKeisha.

"Perfect!" Tamika declared. "He looks a lot better than Geno huh?"

"Hell yeah he do," LaKeisha agreed. "I told you he wasn't nothing but a bitch anyway, now he a pretty bitch. Look at that booty...you better watch out Darnell, them boys gonna be all over that ass. Ha-ha-ha...come on...lets go show him off."

"Naw...not yet, first we gotta teach him to act like a girl," Tamika advised.

"Ha-ha...that won't take long," LaKeisha giggled.

After about an hour of trial and error, Darnell's demeanor was deemed acceptable and the girls marched him straight to the basketball courts on Larkspur Street. They purposely waded through a small crowd of boys they knew would feel them up, then the three of them ran back to Tamika's house giggling and gushing with excitement.

Darnell would never be the same. He spent the rest of that day with Tamika and LaKeisha being a girl. Giggling, talking about boys, especially the ones that had groped them and parading in front of the mirror wearing different outfits and wigs. He even tried on lingerie and absolutely loved the feel of it. From that day on he never again allowed hair to grow on his body or face.

The next day, Darnell honestly admitted to the girls that he loved the experience. All those boys grabbing his ass and trying for more had blown his

mind. He liked the way he looked as a girl. He loved the clothes and the way he felt while wearing them. The whole thing was a total rush but because he feared being recognized, he refused to dress up again unless it was for something really special. And for the first time in his life he refused a direct order from Tamika.

She didn't give up though and after a few days Darnell gave in, dressed as a girl and surprised Aaron who hated it, would have none of it and stormed off much to Darnell's surprise. But within a week LaKeisha had gotten the three of them invited to a dance party given by some students from the nearby Community College. It was being held in the first floor ballroom of the Duncan Hotel and the dress was semi-formal. This Darnell could not resist.

The once grand Duncan Hotel was on its way down. But to those teen-agers from Nelson Park, it was a real big deal. On the day of the dance Tamika sent Darnell on his customary errand to TJs. When Darnell returned LaKeisha and Tamika spent the rest of the day with him smoking grass, dressing and getting ready.

For this occasion the two girls spent considerable time carefully dressing Darnell. After Nuggy's jock strap and two pair of panties came black panty hose, a black stuffed bra then Ruth Ann's silver long sleeved, sequined party dress. The tight fitting dress shimmered and accented Darnell's bouncy prominent round behind. His outfit was completed with black silver trimmed two-inch pumps, a wig of long straight black hair, make-up, jewelry and a black handbag with silver trim. Darnell wore the pumps well because he had bought them the same day he was invited to the party then practiced by wearing the shoes at home. Mostly he had been wearing

the pumps because he liked the way they made his ass bounce. Once again when Tamika and LaKeisha finished their work Darnell was truly a beautiful young woman.

The three of them arrived at the party happy, high on TJs weed and looking good. Tamika and LaKeisha quickly accepted offers to dance, while Darnell was excited and thrilled by the new found male attention. But since he feared being recognized or exposed as a male he accepted only a few offers to fast dance.

Darnell soon discovered he had legitimate access to the women's bathroom and made it a refuge during slow dances. But a fat girl taking a dump forced him to step out of the ladies room during the band's highlight performance, "Wilson Pickett's, I Found a Love, Parts I and II."

Being an attractive young woman at her first dance was a heady experience and Darnell was truly enjoying himself. He leaned against a column and swayed to the music when suddenly a dark muscular arm slid around his waist and a familiar husky voice whispered into his ear. "Goddamn you looking good tonight DARLENE...dance with me baby!"

He had been recognized! Panic and fear gripped Darnell as he whirled around and was shocked. It was Drey! For several days Darnell had been consumed by the rush of being a girl and hadn't even thought about Drey or the possibility of him being at this dance.

He meekly followed as Drey took him by the hand, led him to the dance floor, pulled him close and began slow dancing. Stunned, nervous and excited, Darnell melted into Drey's arms. He glanced around just in time to see LaKeisha leaving with two college-aged

guys while Tamika was at the bar heavily engaged in conversation.

Drey put both hands on Darnell's back, held him tight, nuzzled his ear then whispered, "I really dig you baby, I been digging you all along, but seeing you like this totally fucks me up! Girl...you everything I ever wanted and I mean that shit. You one fine motherfucker tonight Darlene and that's who you are to me baby...DARLENE! And right now YOU MY DARLENE!"

Darnell blinked hard, deep inside he knew this was everything he had secretly longed for...but refused to admit. Now faced with it he simply could not resist Drey...not to mention his words and strong embrace. Darnell was captured, with a girlish sigh he slid his arms around Drey's neck and laid his head on the shoulder of this man he both wanted and feared.

Drey was for real. His ultimate lover would be a small boned, dark-skinned man with delicate features, who dressed as a woman. A fine little woman without all them bitch problems, babies and attitudes. A real pretty boy with a tight round ass and Darlene was perfect. He was one fine little bitch and Drey was thrilled to finally have him in close embrace. His dick had been hard from the moment LaKeisha told him about Darnell coming to the dance dressed as a woman...his woman. Now with Darlene in his arms Drey held him close, kissed his neck, whispered sweet nothings and with one hand lightly massaged Darlene's round ass while they slowly swayed to the music until the song ended. Darnell attempted to pull away but Drey held on to him, kissed him softly on the forehead and whispered, "Let's go outside."

When they reached the parking lot, Drey pulled Darnell into his arms and kissed him full on the lips. Startled, Darnell struggled until he felt Drey's tongue force its way into his mouth. He whimpered, sucked in Drey's tongue, slid his arms around Drey's neck and slowly began grinding his hips. He could feel Drey's hard-on pressing against him, it was big and he wanted...even needed it. Yes! Fuck it...denial was gone, he neded this...he needed Drey's big dick.

Darnell's surrender was total. His hips pushed hard against Drey, hell yes he wanted it. He wanted to stroke and kiss it. His quivering hungry lips were now passionately responding to Drey's kiss, his heart was racing and his own hard dick fought against its constraints. Sexual hunger flooded through Darnell's every fiber as his thoughts overwhelmed him. *Goddamn he wanted it, he wanted to kneel before it, touch it, caress it then suck it, ALL of it. And yes...most of all he wanted every inch of Drey's big hard dick deep inside his virgin ass...even if it hurt!*

For some time Darnell had struggled with this, now he no longer cared. He was totally captured by Drey's pursuit and his own complete surrender. He wasn't sexually hungry...he was absolutely starving! Starving for his true identity and for the touch of his true love. Now he had both. On this night he was not a man and he was not a fag...no he was a woman, a fine sexy woman and it was liberating to finally admit that more than he had ever really wanted anyone in his entire life he truly wanted Drey. He needed to submit to Drey...to be sweet to him...to worship him and be his pussy! Darnell longed to be gentle, delicate and protected, wrapped in the strong arms of this handsome black

man. He looked like a woman, he felt like a woman and at that moment more than anything in the world, Darnell desperately wanted to be Drey's woman. Drey's only woman.

"Let's go to my place," Drey whispered, as he opened his car door. They drove away smiling, feeling on each other, high on expectation and each secretly knowing they were more than a little bit in love with the other.

LaKeisha was mad as a hornet when Drey told her he really dug on Darnell and had fucked him. She was livid and there was no calming her down. No matter what Drey said he could not convince LaKeisha he was not a "low life thrill stealing motherfucker!" She was supposed to have a piece of that action and Drey had cheated her out of it. She didn't care how much Drey really liked Darnell she was totally pissed.

Tamika on the other hand was disappointed. She had wanted to watch Darnell get fucked but it didn't seem to really matter much. Tamika was pre-occupied and over the next few weeks she hardly seemed to notice Darnell, who was now regularly dressing as Darlene and going on dates with Drey.

Chapter eight

For no good reason I could identify my car repair business slowed considerably. I guess the vandals who had been helping me out had moved on. Thing was, now that I had time on my hands both my current lady friends was reneging big time. I kept hearing what sounded to me like phony excuses so I decided to seek some new female company, though I hadn't really got around to that yet. A single man can get mighty lonely if you know what I mean. There is no particular good fortune or joy in living alone. A man that cannot find a mate he can at least slip into mutual toleration with is not a lucky man. He is a man that must keep searching and even as the volume expands, the focus narrows so fewer and fewer make the grade. Unfortunately though, as passions rise standards fall and occasionally that breach can get yo ass in a whole lot of trouble. Believe me I know, so I try and keep my guard up. But neither my guard nor my good common sense was any match for Tamika Martin.

I hadn't seen her for quite some time when she came round knocking on my door. I opened the door

and was shocked. I almost didn't recognize her. She was dressed in expensive clothes and her hair, make-up and nails were professionally done. As homely as she was she looked good.

"Can I come in Uncle Wint?" she beamed then stepped in and twirled around seeming very sure of herself. From her large handbag she produced a small gift-wrapped package. "I brought you a gift, Uncle Wint."

"Why?" I questioned.

"Cause I wanted to, that's why. Here open it," Tamika chuckled.

I opened the gift box and was again shocked as I stared at a very expensive wristwatch. "Girl, where the hell did you get this? It's not hot is it?"

"Ha-ha...I knew you was gonna ask me that," Tamika laughed. "It's legit, here are your registration papers and I got some killer smoke." She lit a joint and put it between my lips. "And I got some killer drink too." Again into the handbag and out with a fifth of Cognac.

"What the hell?" I murmured collapsing into my favorite chair totally astounded.

She fluttered across the room and made two drinks, gave me one, then fluttered across the room again and turned on my stereo. She swayed and danced as she searched through my music collection while I smoked, drank and admired my new time piece not really knowing what to think. After refilling our drinks and starting a new joint, Tamika snuggled up on my couch and for over an hour we talked as never before about a whole range of subjects. I was impressed with her knowledge and maturity and I really enjoyed the conversation, but eventually our talk turned to her

tailored clothes and that expensive wristwatch she had given me.

"I'll explain everything to the last detail," she promised, "But right now...there is something else you should know." She stood up, made new drinks and lit another joint. "I turned eighteen two months ago...that means I'm not a kid anymore Uncle Wint," she announced then started seductively strip dancing. After removing all of her clothes except her panties, she asked, "Can I sit in your lap Uncle Wint? Please?" Totally mesmerized I was in no condition to say no, so she snuggled into my lap and started screwing her bottom around and sighing. She took my hand, kissed my fingers, then looked deeply into my eyes and said, "I love you Uncle Wint. I always have, I always will and this time I'm not gonna be run off. I love you...and I'm in love with you...that's the way it has always been and nothing will ever change that."

She pressed her lips to mine and in all my years I ain't never tasted sweeter. Call it too much booze, call it too much weed, call it too little will power or whatever but...Tamika Martin was just too much and I gave in. I had promised myself I wouldn't but I couldn't stop her and I couldn't stop myself. For a good long time we excitedly kissed away the years of waiting I had insisted upon and it caused me to think she might be right about this. I have always liked this child, hell...even when she was just a little ole baby Tamika was the only child I ever volunteered to baby-sit and Ruth Ann more than eagerly obliged too many times. Now she is a sexy exciting young thing sitting naked on my lap. Her large firm perky titties beckon me while her soft round ass grinds against my crotch. I stroked her hair and looked

managed to suck both nipples at the same time. Tamika moaned loudly and pulled my hair with both hands, prompting me to begin massaging her clit with my fingers. She was responding all over the bed, moaning, sucking in her breath and letting out little shrieks. I let my tongue drift down over her stomach and on to take the place of my fingers. Then suddenly I thought the top of my head was gonna blow off. Without warning her legs slammed around my head. She was clawing the sheets and arching her body upwards, rhythmically grinding her sweet young pussy against my wet hungry tongue. I took my time and let her truly enjoy herself before sliding first one then two fingers into her. I wasn't surprised to find her so wet but I was surprised to find her so tight. She started bucking wildly, slowing for a minute, then wildly bucking again, all the while loudly moaning and cooing, "I love you Winston Littles…I love you so much. Oh god, I swear I do."

After she began to calm down I kissed my way back up her body, pausing on both those firm young nipples again, as I made my way north to her hot, eager, wet and oh so sweet lips. We kissed deep, wet, non-stop grinding, nasty, sloppy, totally fucking into you kisses. When I felt her nails dig into my flesh I raised her legs and slid my hard aching dick into her soft sweet pussy. I just got the head of it in and she gasped, so I backed out then pushed in a little deeper. Goddamn she was tight and good…oh lord she was good. I was only in about two inches but she was tight…so I didn't force it, I just rocked her right there for a while. Then suddenly I started to sink in deeper…and deeper and…oh shit this girl feels so incredibly good! And that look in her eyes…

"Oh! Oh! Oh! Winston…" Tamika cried out.

"Winston...I love you...aww baby..."

I've always been what you might call long-winded when it comes to sex and that night was no exception. We rocked it for a good long time before I finally came. She was lying on her back, her legs around me and my dick as deep in her as I could get it. She was excited and working her ass to my rhythm, humping pussy all up and down my rigid dick. When she shuddered and began moaning, "Oh Winston! Baby? I'm gonna cum...oh...ohhhh!" It was too much and I came too! Goddamn, I mean I really came. Never have I cummed that hard, that long or that good! Thrilled, exhausted and speechless we drifted into a beautiful afterglow. She kissed me repeatedly as I quietly gave thanks to the good lord for this beautiful gift, while holding her close before contentedly dozing off.

I awoke with a sharp pain in my dick...Tamika was doing her best at giving me a blowjob. I was surprised that she really didn't know how but with gentle patience I guided her through the finer points of satisfying this man anyway. She learned quickly and I totally floated in the ecstasy her hot eager mouth provided. Then I turned her around and completed the sweetest sixty-nine known to mankind.

After countless moments in this heaven I entered her again. More easily this time, though I was no less hard and she was no less wet. Over many long wonderful moments the rhythm and positions changed but the thrill, the joy and the passion grew hotter and hotter until Tamika exploded. Then exploded again...and again...each more powerful than the last. I could feel her pussy contracting against my dick and I couldn't stand it. It all felt so good! We clung to each

other, cumming, kissing and feeling great as we soared and snuggled until we again fell asleep.

I awoke the second time to the smell of coffee and bacon. It was morning and Tamika had cooked my breakfast. Wearing my robe she entered the bedroom carrying a tray and I sat up. She looked so sweet and innocent I felt guilty and ashamed of last night. I was mentally fumbling trying to think of a way to freeze this relationship before it gets any deeper. I was also trying to hide my morning hard-on.

"Good morning lover," Tamika beamed. "I'm so excited; you have made me the happiest woman on earth. Here eat your breakfast then we'll talk, and then I'm gonna ride the cum right outta you."

Normally I don't eat breakfast but this morning I was starved. The food was delicious and I gobbled up everything on the tray while Tamika watched with adoring eyes. When I finished eating she took the tray to the kitchen then came back and sat on the side of the bed.

"Now, I got to apologize for something. To be honest, I'm not really sorry, but I promise I will never do it again," she began.

"Tamika, what in the world are you talking about?" I questioned.

"Well I have sort of controlled your life over this past year and I hope you won't be mad at me," Tamika confessed.

"What do you mean you have controlled my life?" I asked with a disbelieving smile.

"Well, almost a year ago you weren't doing much. You had even started hanging with them old men out front, so I rounded up my boys and started doing cars.

They thought we were just having fun but I knew we were creating business for you and you got real busy too. Then after awhile when I knew you had some money put back, I decided you was working much too hard so we stopped doing cars. But then you had time on your hands again. So I had to buy off them two women you were screwing. I sure hope they didn't tell you they loved you Winston cause it only took a few hundred dollars to buy them off," Tamika declared.

"What? You lying!" I challenged.

"Naw I'm not!" Tamika insisted. "I paid Lucille three hundred and I paid Anita five. Then I had my spies watching you and I bought or chased off every woman making eyes at you."

"You expect me to believe that?" I questioned.

"It's the truth! You haven't got any in the last three months have you?" Tamika questioned with a smile. "I apologize Winston, I really do," she continued, "but you made it clear that if I didn't do something our time would never come."

"Well I'll be damned! This shit is too hard to believe. You on the level here Tamika?"

"It's the truth Winston, I swear?" Tamika promised.

"Well kiss my ass...where you getting all this money young lady?"

"The GHC," Tamika grinned.

"Where?"

"You know the GHC. I'm sure you've heard of it," Tamika responded proudly. "It was my idea, well really I got the basic idea from one of Aaron's gay magazines but I set it up. It's all mine and you won't believe how much money I make."

"The GHC? I heard some talk about it but I don't really know what it is. Why don't you tell me about it," I prodded.

"I'll show it to you, it's right here in the building. I'll just take you down there and show you," Tamika promised. "But first!" She took off her robe then pulled back the blanket that had been covering me.

"Now wait a minute Tamika," I ordered.

"No way Winston Littles I have waited years for this!" she replied.

Tamika was one very happy young lady. She was glowing as she stroked my hard-on, then climbed on top of me, covered my mouth, neck and ears with wet kisses, while she rubbed her pussy against my dick till one was sloppy wet and the other was rock hard. We both cried out when she slid my throbbing manhood inside her wet, tight, hot…and I DO mean HOT pussy.

"Oh yes…my sweet baby!" I cried out. At that particular moment I knew I loved this girl…she is way past the best…and I'm gonna keep her! Oh yeah this is definitely mine! The feelings this girl excites in me I cannot explain. I have never had these kinda feelings before and I really do like them. It's a little like finally having sex for the first time. Our love is so fucking hot and exciting. Shit…her touch, her smell, her kiss, her voice, everything about her excites me…makes my body tingle and my dick harder. I don't know how long we fucked that morning but for me fucking don't get no sweeter. I lay on my back and Tamika sit astride me. Beautiful, soft, naked, sweet young girl sitting on top of me…with my dick in her pussy and love in her eyes…it just don't get no better. Our hearts beat as one…and the heavens smiled…as true to her word…my sweet, young

Tamika cried out in ecstasy then passionately rode the cum out of happy ole me.

Chapter nine

*T*HE GLORY HOLE CLUB was the official name
of the "GHC". It was located in apartment 2G right here
in the building. Like most apartments in this building
2G was a shotgun style arrangement, a long row of
rooms one beside the other. You entered into a large
living room next to a smaller dining room with a
hallway leading to the rest of the apartment. 2G had
long been empty and in need of serious repair when
Tamika rented it unofficially. To make the place work
for her she had it crudely remodeled by having three
walls built.

The first wall stretched right across the living
room and sealed off the remainder of the apartment. It
contained a large two-way mirror on the end with a
small slot in it and a large doorway in the middle. The
second and third walls were built across the dining
room about four feet behind the first wall. Into these
walls were built four completely private booths about
three feet wide and about four feet deep. On the back
wall of each booth was a little slot at eye level and at
crotch level was the glory hole. It was about three inches

around, built to accommodate even the biggest penis and the reinforced wall was thin so nearly all of the customer's penis could be serviced. There was an optional step for short dudes and two shoulder level handles for gripping protruded from the wall.

Customers followed a simple procedure at the GHC. To gain entrance you rang the doorbell then wait for the buzzer to unlock the door. Once inside the customer was required to push their ticket to glory through the small slot in the mirror (a large red arrow with the words "insert ticket here" printed on the mirror pointed to the slot). Once a ticket was received through the slot, the clerk behind the mirror delivered a hard plastic card with a door number printed on it back through the slot to the customer. If the GHC was busy the customer would receive the plastic card and a wait number with instructions to have a seat and wait for their number to be called. Otherwise the customer would proceed directly to the door number on the plastic card. Inside the booth a large red arrow with the words "insert card here" printed on it pointed to the slot. A smaller red arrow with the instruction to "put it here for your trip to glory" pointed to the hole. Once the specially indented card was pushed through the slot it released the cap that covered the glory hole. Guide your dick through the hole, grab the handles and hold on for a first class blowjob. Thus the name THE GLORY HOLE CLUB or the GHC.

It was simple, efficient, anonymous and no money was exchanged. The customer entered the GHC, got what they came for and left without any conversation or seeing anyone, except perhaps another customer. The rest of apartment 2G could only be

entered by another unmarked door. The back bedroom was the office. It contained a desk, a couple of chairs and three video monitors, one for the front ticket collection booth and two for the "suck room". The suck room was the back side of the dining room wall containing the booths. It looked like a wide hallway with a small opening on the end leading to the ticket booth. Along the wall were four slots above the glory holes with a stool in front of each one and four lights along the top of the wall directly over each hole. This light stayed on as long as the booth was occupied.

I knew she was intelligent but I have no idea when Tamika matured enough to put this together. She was an astute business woman indeed! Baby meant business. She had TICKETS TO GLORY professionally printed with a special design that made counterfeiting very difficult. Even if you did manage to get in, you could not get any action at the GHC without a ticket. You never saw an employee and you could not buy a Ticket to Glory at the GHC. They were however sold all over the neighborhood. Even Wilson's Variety Store and The Playmore Lounge sold Tickets to Glory. Tamika had bartered Tickets to Glory for the rent, construction, security, printing and any other services she needed. To service customers she hired only certified cum freaks. Those more interested in dicks than money. Her employees included, Darnell who mostly worked in the ticket booth, LaKeisha, Aaron, a little dark girl called Dot, a long-haired white boy named Avery, and to my surprise, Lester. All totaled she had ten dick suckers employed, four females and six males. She sold Tickets to Glory in quantities only at wholesale, allowing the resellers their mark-up and insuring continuing

business. From this revenue she met her payroll and cleared several hundred dollars a week, most of which she saved.

To say the least, I was shocked, impressed and amazed. Maybe I didn't really know Tamika as well as I thought. After all this had sunk in I just had to ask Tamika how come she had done such a poor job on me if she ran a blow job business. She laughed and told me she never had any intention of sucking some strange dick poked through a wall. She was the owner and manager...sucking was not her job. She went on to inform me the video monitors were for security and to observe operations. Tamika's interest was strictly financial and we finished our tour of the GHC by meeting her strong box. She called this thing "Promise Number Three" and it held all of her savings in cash. She gave me a key and insisted on moving it to my apartment.

My mind was blown...I mean completely blown! I didn't know what to think...all this was just too damn much. I needed time to absorb all that Tamika had brought my way and I was thankful that she had to hurry off and was busy with school and her business. She only visited twice over the next week but each visit lasted all night and was oh so special.

A couple mornings later I was having some coffee and herb while trying to sort this shit out when a knock came on the door. I opened it and Ruth Ann marched in.

"You goin tuh jail mutherfuckah!" she declared.

"What?" I questioned.

"Don't whut me, goddamnit! You heard me...yo old ass is goin tuh jail!" Ruth Ann insisted.

"Now wait a minute Ruth Ann!" I ordered.

"Wait muh mutherfuckin ass! Dere's laws gainst fuckin chrilren and yo ass is goddamn sho goin tuh jail!" Ruth Ann belligerently snapped.

"Now look Ruth Ann, I think you have got some bad information," I offered.

"Aw…you ain't been fuckin Tamika huh?" Ruth Ann shot back. "You knows goddamn well you has…and da way ah sees it you gots two choices heah. One marry Tamika or two gos tuh jail and dat's it!" she concluded.

"Ruth Ann you haven't thought this thing out. Ain't neither one of them no good solution to this situation," I advised.

"Oh deys not huh? And just why da fuck is dat!" Ruth Ann questioned.

"Well," I responded, "cause first the age of consent is eighteen or younger not twenty-one like you think. And if I did marry Tamika, which I'm not, you would lose her as a dependent and your welfare check would get a lot smaller. Second since I ain't got no record, even if you did find a way to get me arrested, I'd probably get probation or something like that and Tamika would never forgive you."

"You thanks yo ass is smart don't cha, Mistah mutherfuckah!" Ruth Ann wailed. "Well ah'll tell you one goddamn thang you gots to pay. You heah me! Don't thank ah'm gonna let dis shit just slid by. Aw naw…you can't make no babies! Can you old mutherfuckah? So ain't no welfare money comin for Tamika's baby cause yo old ass can't make none…and you got her nose all fucked up so she ain't likely fuckin nobody else. So ah tells you whut…ah better start seeing some moneys and ah don't mean no chump change

either! You heah me Winston Littles? Ah better start seeing some regular moneys from yo old ass."

She slammed my door behind her and I fixed myself a drink, a big drink, a real big drink.

Chapter ten

*A*mazingly *things seemed to quiet down* as quickly as they had heated up. The next couple months were really very pleasant. Even Ruth Ann had chilled out…at least she hadn't been back to my door. I wasn't paying her anything either and she didn't spare the dirty looks when our paths crossed. Tamika began visiting more often and I became somewhat comfortable with her. Truth is, she was truly a delight. She brought me real nice presents, she cooked…pretty damn good too…she cleaned, fussed over me and made the sweetest love known to mankind, wearing my old ass out in the process and I just loved it. Still though I didn't really know how to define this relationship. Tamika was very effective at warning off any other woman and I tolerated that because I kinda suspected she would soon burn out and move on. A couple of times I even gave some thought to skimming a few bucks out of ole Promise Number Three but didn't, I knew Tamika was too sharp for that. That girl knows to the dollar how much is in that strong box so I've never touched it. In fact I've never even looked at it since that day I lugged the heavy son-

of-a-bitch up here.

Over at the GHC Tamika installed video recorders in her office and began taping the activity in the suck room. At first we would watch some of the action together. For me it was entertainment but Tamika took notes and after a while she started splicing some of the hotter scenes together. She worked on this thing for weeks, consciously making a very serious adult videotape and the arrangements to market it. I had long since lost interest in her suck room tapes when she came bursting through my door with a carton of professionally labeled and packaged videotapes.

"Here it is," she declared. "And I got a ten thousand dollar advance! Five thousand in cash and a five thousand-dollar cashier's check...anyway here it is! A totally unique and innovative adult tape, that's what the agency said. It's going to be sold all over the country and I get a little piece of each sale. I got a gross...that's twelve cases of twelve each or one hundred and forty-four tapes to sell in the neighborhood and I get all of that."

She was all aglow, proud, beaming, on cloud nine and I was proud of her. It was one hell of an accomplishment and once again I was deeply impressed. I opened a bottle of champagne while Tamika put the tape into the VCR and we settled back to watch her creation. *"The Dicks of Nelson Park", produced and directed by TRM.* The tape began with a close shot of one of the little doors covering the crotch level hole in the wall, then suddenly the door snapped open and a hard brown dick came through the hole. The shot widened out as LaKeisha rolled up on her stool and performed a masterful blowjob on it.

Another close shot of a glory hole snapping open and certainly the biggest dick I have ever seen pushed through. That dick must have been twelve inches long and it wasn't completely hard. A wide shot showed Dot, Avery, LaKeisha and Lester all racing to service that monster. Dot got there first. She pushed the stool away, bent over, placed both hands on the wall and swallowed as much dick as she could. She was grinding her hips as she tried mightily to deep throat this giant, which incredibly was getting even bigger.

Dot was naked so Avery got behind her, slid his hard-on into her hot pussy and let Dot fuck him while she sucked. Dot was enthusiastically servicing both dicks when LaKeisha approached with a Ping-Pong paddle and began smacking Avery on his ass. This rhythmic ass smacking, fucking and sucking kept up for several minutes until the customer abruptly came. Cum ran from the corners of Dot's mouth as she struggled to drink every drop before the huge dick retreated back behind the wall. The glory hole door snapped shut and LaKeisha dropped the paddle then laid back on the floor and pulled Dot's head into her crotch. Dot was on fire. She truly loved all kinds of sex and once she got going she would happily do everybody in the room. She sank to her knees and eagerly licked LaKeisha's pussy while pumping her ass as Avery continued to slide his dick in and out of her. Lester joined the fun by getting on his hands and knees and licking Avery's asshole, prompting Aaron to lie on his back, scoot between Lester's legs and suck his dick. The five of them fell into the same rhythm and fucked, licked and sucked up a storm.

Suddenly two lights came on and two dicks emerged through the wall. There was a mad scramble to

get to and service these dicks. The remaining two lights lit up and soon four of the five were seated on their stools happily sucking a strange dick.

"I charge them for fucking and they don't seem to mind," Tamika chuckled.

"You charge who?" I questioned.

"My staff, LaKeisha, Dot, Lester, all of them," Tamika responded. "Anybody who gets sucked or fucked at the GHC has to pay. That's why I started recording the suck room to begin with. I watch the tapes and take notes then dock their pay. I give them a fifty percent discount and they have never complained once."

"Did you pay them to be in the movie?" I asked.

"Are you kidding?" Tamika laughed. "I told them the tape is being sold nationwide and they could become movie stars. First I had them sign releases with real and phony names, then I gave each of them three copies of the tape and you should have seen them smile. Hey…they are happy to be movie stars!"

The tape was now showing Dot with her back on her stool, legs and ass flat against the wall giving some lucky customer pussy instead of head.

"That's one of her favorite tricks," Tamika sighed, "LaKeisha too. Dot gave up so much one week; I had to stop docking her so she would get some pay anyway."

The scene on the tape again shifted, Lester was on his hands and knees with his lips pressed to the glory hole. As he slowly backed away a thick white dick slipped from his mouth and backed out of the glory hole. Lester licked his lips as the cap snapped back over the hole. Again a scene shift and a very small and obviously very young dick emerged through the wall. Aaron and Dot took turns lovingly sucking it. Another

scene shift and again all the holes are filled with dicks and all the mouths are busy sucking.

Raw hard core sex was filling the screen and I was enjoying the tape but a troublesome question began nagging at me. "Is this tape being sold in the neighborhood?" I asked.

"Sure," Tamika replied, "It's already out there. In fact I've sold out. All the people who sell tickets to glory are also selling the tape. I've only got this one case left and I collect up front. So…yeah the tapes are sold and Promise Number Three is fat and getting fatter…hee-hee."

"Do your movie stars know this tape is being sold down the street?" I inquired.

"Sure…I guess I told them nationwide," Tamika responded.

"Tamika…do your customers at the GHC know that many of the blowjobs are given by men?" I questioned.

"I don't know, but what difference does that make? A blowjob is a blowjob, right?" Tamika challenged.

"Maybe…but some of them may not be too happy to find out a fag has been sucking them off," I suggested.

"Well we haven't had any complaints, not one…and they can't see who's sucking them anyway, so why should they care?" Tamika theorized.

"I hope I'm wrong but you may lose a few customers behind this," I advised.

"You know you may be right about that Winston but I can afford to lose a lot of customers with the money I've already made on this tape," Tamika replied with a big smile as the tape ended and she began

undressing.

"Winston would you like to fuck LaKeisha, or Ruby or Dot or any of the guys on my staff? They will do anything I tell them too so it's no problem."

"No way baby all I want is you," I assured her.

"You sure? Cause I'll do anything to make you happy. They say men like to play around and if that's what you want I'll bring them to you," Tamika promised.

"I've done my playing around little mama and as long as I've got you I don't want or need nobody else! AND I mean that!" I responded.

"I love you Winston Littles, you fine ole dog," Tamika beamed. "Can I ask you something?"

"Sure!"

"You won't get mad?" she asked.

"No. Why should I get mad over a question?" I responded.

"Cause it's a sensitive question," Tamika advised.

"So, go for it," I replied nonchalantly.

"Okay...am I as good in bed as my mama?" she asked.

"Whoa...I wasn't ready for that one," I admitted.

"It's okay if you don't want to answer," Tamika replied.

"Naw...naw...that's cool...straight up...you asked and I'll answer. I haven't been with your mama in several years, so I don't know what she's like in bed now," I honestly replied. "Way back when though she was pretty good, but at her best she wasn't half as good as you."

"How did she like to do it?" Tamika asked.

"Doggie style, that was her thing, on all fours," I

replied.

"Did she suck you off or want you to eat her out?" Tamika questioned.

"She tried but she wasn't worth a shit at it cause she wasn't really into that," I responded.

"What was she into...I mean what really turned her on?" Tamika asked.

"You sure you really want to hear this?" I questioned.

"Yes I do sweetheart more than you know," Tamika assured.

"Okay," I sighed, "ass fucking she loved dick up her butt."

"Really?" Tamika gushed.

"Oh yeah, if you didn't fuck Ruth Ann in the butt you wasn't shit in her book. And better for you if you spanked that ass first," I replied remembering but one of the reasons I had tired of Ruth Ann.

"Will you fuck me in my butt?" Tamika asked without hesitation.

"You sure you wanna do that?" I inquired with some concern.

"I'm sure," Tamika responded in a confident tone.

"Ever done that before?"

"No...why?"

"Cause it may hurt a little especially the first time," I advised.

"I don't care if it does hurt, you are my man and I want every inch of you buried deep in my ass...end of story."

She smiled covered my mouth with a long wet kiss then hungrily began sucking my dick. I lubricated two fingers with Vaseline and slowly, gently began

massaging them deep into her tight little butt. She giggled when I told her to grease my dick but she done an excellent job, then rose to her knees, lowered her shoulders to the floor and raised her beautiful young brown butt into the air. I savored her soft round ass, spread her cheeks and slowly pushed my nice friendly dick into her. When the head entered her asshole she gasped and tightly gripped it, then released it to slide in a little deeper. Breathing hard but determined to do this, she slowly relaxed and I began lovingly stroking. It was so beautiful seeing my hard dick slide in and out of her and watching her ass rise to meet me.

"Does it hurt baby?" I asked.

"Yes! But no, no...it hurts but it's kinda good too. Oh shit your thing is huge...oh...awww. Don't stop, I'm gonna take it...all of it...at least this once. Oh God Winston...fuck me good...I love you...I love you baby..." Tamika responded.

I put my arm around her and touched my fingers to her clit, setting off the wildest ride I can remember. She pumped her ass so furiously she knocked me off balance and I fell over on my side. I held on to her, pushed my hard dick even deeper into her tight butt, clamped my fingers onto her pussy and rocked her young world a good long while. The cum started to build as she ground her ass against me and I pumped in and out. Grunting, pumping and sweating until I exploded again and again, shooting loads of hot cum deep into her ass. Tamika went totally rigid, then began squeezing my dick with her ass muscles and it really felt good. Finally we lay motionless and quiet for several long moments.

Tamika washed both of us then lit a joint. She

snuggled into my arms and asked, "Am I better than Ruth Ann?"

"Baby everything about you is a million times better than Ruth Ann. Ruth Ann's best can't match your worst," I responded.

"You just saying that to please me Winston?" she asked.

"Hell no, I don't have to lie. If Ruth Ann was half as good as you we would have never stopped kicking it in the first place," I honestly replied.

"How am I so much better than she is? She's got way more experience!" Tamika questioned.

"That's a big part of it," I explained. "Experience doesn't necessarily make a woman better. Quite frankly sometimes it just makes her mind callused and her pussy loose in more ways than one. I never once thought of Ruth Ann as being sweet or special. I never once thought Ruth Ann was all mine. But I know you are and that makes all the difference in the world. You're sweet, you're very, very special and you're mine."

"Can I ask you something?" Tamika asked with a gleam in her eye.

"Sure," I responded.

"I've never known you to lie or run a game but what about when you first moved in here and all those women were trying to have your baby?" she questioned.

"Ha-ha-ha...well kiss my ass...you done your homework! Ha-ha-ha," I chuckled with a bit of embarrassment then asked, "Who told you about that? Ha-ha-ha..."

"Wanda," Tamika replied.

"Ahh ha-ha-ha...Wanda...who else but...ha-ha-ha. Truth is baby," I confided, "not one of those women

asked me if I wanted to...or if I could make a baby. Not one! Ha-ha-ha...and I would have told them if they had asked...Ha-ha-ha..."

"You knew they were trying to get pregnant?" Tamika questioned in surprise.

"Course I knew...ha-ha. But what the hell I was young...had fun...ha-ha."

"Yeah way I heard it you had big fun," Tamika teased.

"Yeah, fun back then but it don't compare to now. I'd trade all that for you in a heartbeat cause you inside my head little mama! No woman has ever...or will ever...even get close to the special way you make me feel. I love you...but I can't truly explain these feelings cause they all brand new to me." I lifted my sweetheart's chin to kiss her but her eyes were full of tears, so I picked her up and took her to bed.

Chapter eleven

Within two days Tamika's video "The Dicks of Nelson Park" hit like a bullet. It sold out immediately in the neighborhood and Nelson Park was all-abuzz. There had always been rumors and now the videotape confirmed them. The GHC was full of fags, queers and freaks. This particular group of people is not tolerated well out in the open, not in this community anyway, so the GHC was trashed.

Late one evening some revenge seekers painted the words "Punk Ass Fag Motherfuckers" on the front door then kicked it open, sending the office worker and all five dick suckers scrambling out the back entrance and up to my apartment.

They came through my front door out of breath and scared. LaKeisha, Andre and Dot were naked. Ruby, Darnell and Michael were dressed. Tamika was in my apartment at the time and she was at first terrified then angry. My concern was for Tamika, so to calm everyone down I used our only available diversion. Tamika offered clothes to the naked but I suggested we all get naked instead. No sex...just a little independent island

of freedom in the mist of a very funky storm. They were safe here...we couldn't exactly call the cops, so fuck it! Lets just kick back, get loose and relax while we wait this shit out. That rap plus a joint for each of them from my primo stash worked and restored a sense of calm.

We undressed, sat on the floor in kinda of a semi-circle and relaxed, smoked, drank, ate, told jokes, napped, played cards, laughed and escaped an otherwise very unpleasant night. I kept our party going until sunrise. Funny how being naked relaxes and liberates people, even perverts. We were all feeling pretty good when I knew the time had come to return to reality. So we all dressed and paid a cautious visit to Apartment 2G, The GHC.

The Glory Hole Club was destroyed and stripped. Everything was taken...the VCRs, cameras, monitors, desk, furniture, even the ticket collection box and the light bulbs. Messages were spray painted on the walls, things like "Sissy fag motherfuckers" and "Suck my 9mm Punk" or "Fuck the GHC".

Tamika raced from room to room then gathered her staff and said, "Well folks...as you can see, the Glory Hole Club is closed. It ceased to be at the close of business yesterday...you will be paid up to that date. You can pick up your final pay at Winston's place anytime after two o'clock this afternoon. This place and you guys were good...really good! This was real while it lasted. We had a great run and I really want to thank each of you for just being yourself and making this all work. Someday...somehow...we will be back, bigger and better than this...and I do mean you can count on that! As for anymore about the GHC...it never existed! I have never heard of a GHC or Glory Hole Club and I

know nothing at all about it! Is that clear? Okay...thanks again...now go on home...see you tomorrow...I mean later today...okay? Bye now."

When we got back to my apartment Tamika collapsed into my arms. She was hurt, scared, angry and confused. I hurt for her while she sat in my lap and I kissed her tears away. By the time the first of her staff arrived for their final pay, Tamika and I had grieved the demise of the GHC, had sex, breakfast, a nap and were going for yet more sex. The first to knock on the door was that totally queer and obvious fag, Michael. He was rabbit scared and fidgeted the whole time he was here. He's such an all out chicken-shit punk I just don't like him. Tamika paid him and I was glad to see my front door hit him in his queer ass. A steady stream followed him and Tamika's mood brightened considerably.

The following evening first Darnell then LaKeisha finally came to my apartment for their pay and by the time they left Tamika was more scared and depressed than ever. They reported that while walking across the park Aaron got an ass whipping severe enough to send him to the hospital. Another GHC employee named Keith got hit in the eye but his fast feet saved his ass from further harm. Avery was chased for blocks and never returned to the Nelson Park Apartments while Lester was busy moving his unsuspecting common-law wife and family to Washington Heights. Both Dot and Ruby were forced to give more than one public blowjob, but LaKeisha escaped this humiliation by carrying and using a .32 caliber pistol. At least two lives were spared only by her poor aim. Word around the park was there was still a score to settle. Most didn't believe Tamika was really

behind the GHC but thought she knew who was and a few fools were looking for her.

Despite my assurances that she was in no danger, for the next few weeks Tamika absolutely refused to leave my apartment even to go home. LaKeisha and Darnell ran her errands but despite Tamika's objections, I came and went as usual. Some of them damn fools around Nelson Park actually thought I was really behind the GHC. And a couple of them even got in my face. One insisting his old lady recognized his dick on the tape and he felt like I owed him something. I told him point blank, I wouldn't put my dick through a blind wall for free and I sure as hell wasn't gonna waste my time talking to some damn fool that has been paying good money to do just that. I don't owe nobody shit but a bullet if you come fucking with Tamika or me. They knew I meant it and I never heard nothing else about the GHC.

Tamika meanwhile spent the weeks of her seclusion doting on me. Been a real long time since I had a live-in woman and I was really beginning to like having her around. But crossing the courtyard one day, I ran into Ruth Ann. I think she was waiting on me.

"Ain't you been furgettin somethin lately, old mutherfuckah?" she demanded.

"What!" I snapped.

"Don't whut me!" she shot back. "You know whut da fuck ah mean! You bettah git caught up too...befo dis weekend goddamnit! Da jails still open!"

I didn't know what Ruth Ann was talking about and I didn't care but it sorta nagged at me, so I told Tamika about it.

"Oh! I forgot all about mama...damn! Well that's

okay, I'll take care of it," Tamika promised.

"What do you mean you'll take care of it?" I inquired. "What's been going on?"

"Well mama went kind of nuts when she found out about us," Tamika informed me. "She threatened to have you put in jail and kept screaming you gots to pay. So every two weeks I put one hundred dollars in an envelope and slid it under the door when I knew she was home. She just assumed the money was from you. But after the GHC got took out, I just spaced her out. But don't worry, Promise Number Three is still fat, so I can buy mama off."

I didn't agree I wasn't gonna pay Ruth Ann shit and I didn't want Tamika to pay her anything either. We agreed to wait a couple of weeks and talk about it again. The very next week though, I looked up while working on a car and spotted Ruth Ann talking to some white woman in business clothes. Ruth Ann pointed in my direction more than once and that did it. For the first time in my life I truly felt cornered, between a rock and a hard place. I was not about to be dictated to nor was I gonna answer any questions about my relationship with Tamika. So the very next morning Tamika left my apartment for the first time in several weeks. The two of us went to City Hall and got a marriage license. I told myself and a smiling Tamika the sole reason for this was to bluff Ruth Ann.

Chapter twelve

That marriage license gave Tamika a newfound freedom. She went home and waved it around like it was the American flag then moved most of her stuff to my place and quit school. Ruth Ann to say the least was stunned and I was knocked off balance myself but Tamika seemed to know exactly what she was doing. She even talked me into buying her an engagement ring. As far as she was concerned we were but a ceremony away from being man and wife and that would fulfill her fourth and final promise.

Little did I know that at the age of twelve Tamika made herself four solemn promises and she had been driven to fulfill them ever since. The first promise was to identify her father. The second promise was to never have a baby. The third was to become wealthy and the fourth was to become Mrs. Winston Littles. She was always one step ahead...she knew it and loved it.

Over the next couple weeks Tamika spent considerable time looking out the window of my living room and making notes. From that window you could see the few seedy shops still in business on Larkspur

Street. Wilson's Variety Store, Big Daddy's Bar-B-Que, Flo's Beauty Shop and a pool room called Jimmies Joint were the only businesses left in that whole block. Occasionally she used my binoculars and whenever I asked what she was looking at her answer was always the same, "I'm researching my next move...can I get you something honey? No? Then can I have a hug?"

After a short while Tamika enrolled in beauty school and that really pleased me. I had been very concerned about her dropping out of high school but a trade made a world of difference. I even drove her across town to school and picked her up every day. Before she was halfway through beauty school, Tamika had talked LaKeisha, Darnell, Aaron, Lester, Avery and Dot into enrolling into the same school. Little did any of them know Tamika had gotten a sizable new student referral fee from the school for each of them. Though she was nowhere near the top of her class she did graduate and immediately went to work at Flo's Beauty Shop. I was impressed and pleased with her even though I knew Tamika was one lousy beautician. She didn't really like it and had little patience with fussy old ladies. But she had spotted an opening, developed a plan and followed it to the letter.

It only took Tamika four months from the day she joined the staff to produce a videotape of Flo in bed with a well hung young stud named Maurice and Tamika's brother Sam. Flo or Florence Johnson, the wife of an Elder at the Gladstone Street Missionary Baptist Church, was a prominent citizen in several social circles. She was a matronly middle-aged woman with silver hair and a no-nonsense attitude. Sister Florence Johnson was the last woman in town I would expect to see on videotape

in bed with two young lions but there she was in living color. Tamika used this tape to buy the beauty shop from Flo at a ridiculous price. She paid in cash, got the proper legal papers and Florence Johnson stayed on as head beautician.

No one lost their job during Tamika's takeover. In fact the staff doubled in size very quickly. The reason Tamika went to beauty school and worked four months as a beautician was to learn then acquire the business. Tamika never had any intention of being a beautician one day longer than it took to become the owner and manager of her own salon. This young lady liked to work with her head, not her hands; so on the day she took ownership of the shop she stopped being a beautician forever.

Her talent and love was management and she was damn good at it. Tamika was smart, irresistibly charming and ruthless as hell. Her business plan laid out a series of goals, priorities and time frames. Right away she leased the vacant store next to her beauty shop. The adjoining wall was removed doubling the size of the place and the whole shop was remodeled. Her new shop was called "Tamika's Total Hair Care" and it was set up to service both men and women. She encouraged her former GHC staff members to study different specialties then hired each one of them as soon as they finished beauty school. I don't know how Tamika knew but every one of them had an easy time in school, learned their trade well and seemed perfectly suited to the beauty and hair business.

Darnell turned out to be a natural hair stylist. While in school he had grown his hair long and straight, down to his shoulders. On his first day at work he

reported to the salon dressed as a woman. He stepped through the front door and announced that he had moved to the eastside, was sharing an apartment with Drey, and his name was now officially Darlene. No one seemed particularly surprised or shocked that Darnell had publicly declared himself to be a woman. In fact, he was such a good-looking woman his change for most was quickly accepted. From that day on, Darnell dressed and acted like a woman, never again dressing or speaking as a man.

Aaron quickly completed all the required courses but extended his stay in beauty school to study his specialty. Nails, hands or feet. Manicures, pedicures and what he termed "Nail Art". He was fast and gentle, really good at it and soon his became the busiest station in the salon. He loved his job and often worked late to accommodate waiting customers or properly tutor his apprentices. He also loved the gay bars and gyms he now hung in after work.

Lester was still living with Wilona in Washington Heights and had quit his job as a hospital orderly shortly before graduating from beauty school. He had fallen in love with the energy and intimacy of the hair and beauty business and was eagerly becoming a very competent full service beautician.

Dot was every bit as good a beautician as Lester but her real talent was make-up. Make-up, makeovers, facials, you name it and Dot could really lay you out. Behind her back folks said she was so good at make-up because she had plenty practice covering the bruises and lumps her old man be putting up side her head. She still lived in Nelson Park with her two kids and her big dumb, sometime boyfriend she loved to fight with.

Although he managed to graduate from beauty school, Avery wasn't particularly great at anything but shampoos, maintaining stock and running errands. He was just a bi-sexual, longhaired white boy that loved black folks, most of which loved him back. Sheila loved him more than most. Sheila Barnett was about thirty-five years old, fat, black and blonde. She wore too much make-up and had been a shampoo and clean-up girl at Flo's Beauty Shop for seven years when Avery was hired. On his first day at work, Sheila discovered that Avery was bi-sexual and twenty-two years old. On his second work day Sheila invited him home after work, for dinner, drugs and freaky sex with her and her husband Woodrow.

Woodrow Barnett was a local delivery truck driver. He was forty-two years old, stood six feet tall and weighed close to two hundred forty pounds. He was big, black, had a gold tooth and greasy straightened hair called a process. The Barnett's had never considered their marital bed to be sacred and over the years had shared it more than once. It was no secret that Sheila had long held a fantasy of having a young, longhaired white boy for a love slave. Occasionally, when he got drunk enough, Woodrow would join Sheila in this fantasy, making her love slave into a bi-sexual they both could fuck at the same time. Though he would never admit it, Woodrow had long wanted to fuck a boy just for the hell of it.

For Sheila the timing was perfect. She knew Woodrow was bored by the way he made love. So that night she fed him a good dinner, played around in ways she knew would get him aroused, got him plenty high then told him about Avery, their fantasy come to life.

The more they talked about freaking with a white boy love slave the more excited they became. Finally they agreed to live out their fantasy and live it to the MAX!

After he accepted her invitation, Avery and Sheila were like two love struck teenagers the rest of their workday. But, when they arrived at the Barnett's house, Woodrow was waiting and he laid down the law. Avery was to be their complete and total slave. He was to call them Massa and Missus and do exactly as he was told. He was never to make eye contact or talk back. Refuse an order and get a serious ass whipping then sent home.

Excited and all aglow, Avery quickly agreed and completed the first order from his Massa. He completely stripped and put on a small lace apron and waitress cap then made drinks and rolled joints for his Massa and Missus. He served dinner, made more drinks, rolled more joints, cleaned up the dinner dishes and made more drinks. Woodrow put a collar around his neck, hooked a leash to it and walked him around the living room like a dog. His Massa let Avery make himself a big strong drink then ordered him to pour it into a doggie bowl and drink like a dog. Avery lay at their feet all hunched up like a dog while the Barnett's petted his head, called him Avery Boy and threw joint butts on the floor for him to snarf up.

Avery's head was spinning and his heart was beating fast. He loved this shit. He couldn't even dream up some shit this good. He was now the personal white slave for two big, beautiful, aggressive and very threatening black people. He saw Sheila as an overbearing yet motherly, dark, dusky furnace of sexual heat and pleasure. While Woodrow was clearly the superior, intimidating, dominant black dick he

absolutely worshipped and totally adored. Father...lover...ruler...and supreme abuser! No one and no thing less than an act of God could have pried Avery away from the Barnetts that evening.

Woodrow ordered slave Avery to undress Sheila. It took Woodrow a long time to get hard and a long time to get off. To his credit Avery could get off several times and Sheila would happily take all the dick she could get.

When Avery finished undressing Sheila, she ordered him to suck her big titties then smacked him on the face when his teeth grazed her nipple. "Suck it like a baby foe I kicks yo white ass! Dat's better...uh huh...now lights me a cigarette...den git over dere and undress yo Massa Woodrow...and hang dem goddamn clothes up too...git to it boy!" she demanded.

Avery got to his chores. He worked quickly but when he pulled down Woodrow's shorts and saw his dick he froze. It was big, black, thick, meaty and not even semi-hard. Avery desperately wanted to suck it. He almost reached out for it but Woodrow caught on and tormented him.

"You wants to taste dis black meat don't cha white boy? Don't you touch it! Don't you touch it! Aw naw...don't you dare! Stay on your knees boy!" Woodrow waved his dick close around Avery's face, touching it to his chin and cheeks. Then rubbed it across Avery's mouth but ordered him to keep his lips shut, which caused Avery's eyes to water with desire. "Git over there and suck Missus Sheila's pussy...do a good job on that and ah might let you taste some of dis fine black meat heah...ha-ha," Woodrow chuckled.

"Hang them clothes up first and makes us fresh drinks," Missus Sheila ordered.

Avery hopped to it, even making himself a drink and pouring it into his doggie bowl. Missus Sheila was sitting on the couch as Avery approached on his hands and knees. She reached out and grabbed his head pulling him down on her pussy. Avery knew how to eat pussy and was good at it. In no time Missus Sheila was pulling his hair and babbling.

Woodrow was also having a good time…he smiled and stroked his dick. It made him feel good to see Sheila getting off and enjoying herself. Thinking about what he was gonna do to Avery made his dick start to rise so after Sheila began to settle down he again spoke. "Okay…you serviced her pretty good white boy…reckon you done earned a taste of dis dick…so crawl yo ass on over here."

Avery backed off Missus Sheila and turned to obey but Woodrow stood up, grabbed the leash and pulled Avery's face level to his dick. "See dat dick boy, its one of yo big responsibilities…it ain't hard just yet, but you gonna take care of that…ain't you boy?" he questioned.

"Yassuh! I'd be pleased to!" Avery responded.

"Damn right boy! You gonna suck it off…and drink my cum too when I tells you to…ain't you boy?" Woodrow demanded.

"Yassuh!" Avery replied with enthusiam.

"And when I decides I wants to fuck you…you gonna take dis black dick all da way up yo tight ass ain't cha boy?" Woodrow continued.

"Yassuh!" Avery vowed.

Woodrow was holding his dick with one hand and smacking it across Avery's face as he talked. "Dat ass is tight ain't it?" he questioned.

"Yassuh, real tight," Avery promised.

"Goddamnit it better be!" Woodrow threatened, then smiled and asked, "You likes dis shit don't cha white boy?"

"Yassuh...oh...yassuh!" Avery confirmed.

"You really wants a mouth full of this big ole black dick, don't cha?" Woodrow teased.

"Oh yassuh...I really wants it bad suh," Avery pleaded.

"Open yo mouth den white boy and taste some of dis!" Massa Woodrow commanded with a big grin then slid his dick into the white boy's mouth releasing his hand as his slave took over.

Avery had seriously considered himself to be a professional dick sucker while employed at the GHC. He studied movies, books and live performances taking lessons when and where he could, all in an effort to refine and perfect his oral techniques. Avery had graduated from dick sucking school with honors and at this point in his life was among the best pure dick suckers in town. He could totally spoil a man because his first love was sucking dick...big thick, funky tasting black dick. Juice dripped from Avery's chin as his Massa joyously watched this young white boy suck his entire dick. All of it, every throbbing black inch was happily and passionately being sucked in and out of Avery's hungry mouth. In short order Massa Woodrow was harder than he had been in months.

"Goddamn! You one talented mutherfuckah! Look at dis hard-on Sheila girl!" Woodrow howled, pushing Avery out of the way.

"Oooh shit daddy, let me feel some of that!" Sheila purred then spread her legs and laid back on the couch.

Woodrow wasted no time he quickly shoved his big throbbing meat into Sheila and fucked her hard for a few minutes, while she kept repeating, "Oh daddy, oh daddy, oh daddy!"

Avery was reeling and breathing hard. He wanted his Massuh's dick back in his mouth. He loved the funky taste and feel of it. It was the best! No question this was the best dick he had ever sucked and he had fallen in love. Anxiously he watched his Massuh's broad black ass flex as he vigorously fucked Missus Sheila. Avery squirmed as he thought about his Massas promise to fuck him. He had been fucked in the ass only a few times and never by a dick any bigger than his own. He had a strong desire, perhaps even a need for it but so far had found little satisfaction in taking it up his rear. Avery began to sweat as he found himself wondering if his ass could actually take all of Massa Woodrow's big black meat.

Woodrow pulled out and sat next to Sheila, his dick still hard. "Stand up boy and take that goddamn apron off. Let Missus Sheila see what you got," he ordered.

Avery threw off the apron and exposed his semi-hard dick.

"Beat it...jack it off...git it up boy...show the Missus all yo stuff!" Woodrow demanded.

Avery stroked himself to a respectable hard on. His dick was just about six inches at it's hardest and he looked like a little boy compared to Woodrow. He felt somewhat encouraged when Missus Sheila said, "Dat's a pretty good looking piece of white meat. Come here boy." She leaned forward and sucked Avery's dick for a few moments then held it up for inspection. "That's

better...ain't it Woodrow."

"Yeah and he better know what the fuck to do with it or I'm gonna whup his ass! Back on your knees boy!" Woodrow commanded.

Missus Sheila took the leash and walked her slave to the bedroom. She lay back on her bed and ordered Avery to lay on top of her, then kissed him deeply and passionately. Avery responded in kind, eagerly enjoying his Missus. In between kisses, Sheila spread her legs and ordered Avery to fuck her and he immediately put his hard dick into Missus Sheila's hot, funky pussy. It was wet and he slipped around, but Avery done his best to fuck his Missus.

Massa Woodrow briefly watched then sat next to Sheila on the bed, grabbed Avery's head and stuck his dick into the white boy's mouth. Avery really got into this. He sucked his black Massa and fucked his black Missus with great enthusiasm. A few minutes later Woodrow withdrew his dick from Avery's mouth and stood up. He picked up a thick leather belt and slapped Avery hard across the ass. WAP! Pain and excitement rushed through Avery's body. WAP! Another slap of the leather against Avery's naked ass drove him deeper into Missus Sheila. "WHAT CHA DOING FUCKIN MY WOMAN WHITE BOY?" Woodrow roared. WAP! WAP! Two more hard slaps across Averys reddening ass, as Woodrow again roared, "WHAT YOU DOING FUCKIN MY WOMAN WHITE BOY? HUH? WHAT THE HELL YOU DOING FUCKIN HER?"

"Sh...sh...she...she ordered me too, Massa...Suh!" Avery stammered.

"Well then fuck her good boy!" Woodrow demanded. WAP! "Fuck her good!" WAP! "Give dat

black pussy plenty white dick boy!" WAP! "Fuck her!" WAP! "Fuck her white boy!" WAP! WAP! "Fuck dat pussy!"

Avery was jumping in ten different directions, his ass was stinging and burning and his dick was so hard it hurt. He flopped around on top of Missus Sheila and pumped as hard as he could into her more than ample pussy while she grabbed his head and again forced her tongue deep inside his mouth.

Woodrow greased his dick with Vaseline then roughly thumbed Vaseline into Avery's asshole. He climbed on top of the white boy, who was still on top of his Missus and with one merciless long firm stroke shoved his hard, eleven inch black dick deep into his slave's tight smoldering red ass. Avery screamed as Missus Sheila held his ass cheeks apart while Massa Woodrow slowly fucked him with long firm strokes. Without warning cum exploded from the slave boy's aching hard-on into his Missus and he begin to relax. Releasing that tension allowed his asshole to loosen and deliver waves of perverse pleasure as his Massa kept driving his big meaty dick in and out of Avery's skinny white ass with increasing rhythm and force. Tripping, Avery began to think of himself as the true white cream filling in the perfect human Oreo cookie.

Meanwhile Massa Woodrow got on his knees. He grabbed and raised Sheila's legs forcing his dick deeper into Avery's asshole which caused Avery's dick to push deeper into his Missus. Sheila got a firm hold on Woodrow...and the Barnett's fucked. Oh how they fucked. Woodrow and Sheila were big, hot, excited black people and they put a serious fucking on young white Avery. Every time Woodrow pushed down Sheila

pushed up…they fucked right through Avery. With Woodrow's dick buried deep in his ass and Sheila's pussy swallowing his entire dick, the slave boy couldn't concentrate. Nothing he had ever experienced could compare with this and he was becoming delirious. The Barnett's fucked poor Avery so hard, the boy lost all control and pissed a short stream into his Missus. Sheila was screaming with delight while Avery was clawing the sheets and wailing when Massa Woodrow finally came. He was grinding and rocking so deep and hard inside Avery's ass, the white boy came into Sheila's hard humping pussy for the third time. Woodrow collapsed and the three of them lay in a sweaty heap for several moments, breathing hard and lovingly stroking each other, before a totally spent Avery followed orders to wash his Massa and Missus and change their bed sheets. He was then allowed to sleep on the floor at the foot of their bed, with the understanding that he was to awake before his Massa, fix breakfast and be ready to suck his Massa's morning hard-on. Only then was he permitted to rush home and clean up before going to work.

After many such nights and weekends, Avery and the Barnett's found themselves in love with their game and each other. All three of them wanted to make their arrangement permanent so Avery changed his address and moved his personal belongings to the Barnett's house then legally changed his name from…Averill Hastings Flannigan to "Avery Boy Barnett". He then signed a document pledging to spend the remainder of his life as the personal slave of Woodrow and Sheila Barnett. The Barnett's also both signed the document as owners and guardians of one, "Avery Boy Barnett." Tamika notarized the thing and

they even had an official ceremony in her office, complete with a fake judge who made a big deal out of putting the state seal on the phony document.

A brief reception was held afterwards with a few very close friends and soon the Barnett's and their loving slave hurried home. The spare bedroom was named slave quarters and given to Avery Boy as his personal space, though it contained little in the way of furniture. Avery Boy was ordered to move the single bed from his quarters to the Master bedroom, placing it across the foot of his Massa's king size bed.

Avery Boy Barnett was in a heaven of double love he could not explain. For the first time in his life he truly felt loved and wanted. The Barnett's fulfilled his various needs and gave him a sense of belonging. For many years thereafter he happily spent every night of his life sleeping at the feet of his Massa and Missus, who never tired of their slave.

For me however, the real surprise was LaKeisha. She was a barber and a damn good one. She was also very pregnant and had publicly identified the father as Marshall Ferguson. Marshall, the postman at Nelson Park for many years was getting close to retiring. He had been separated from his wife for about a year and a half and now that she knew he had a young girl pregnant, the shit was hitting the fan.

LaKeisha started teasing Marshall when she was about seventeen. She didn't especially like Marshall but LaKeisha had been well schooled by a favorite aunt and was in search of a sugar daddy. Marshall became her prime candidate when she overheard him joking with another man about stealing panties off the clothesline.

"They'd have to be dirty for me to steal em,"

Marshall laughed. "Good'n funky with the smell of young pussy den they'd be special."

Two days later LaKeisha gave Marshall a little gift-wrapped box. It contained one pair of her most dainty panties heavily stained with her most recent pussy juice. Marshall flipped and gave her money for more. It quickly became Marshall's thing to collect LaKeisha's dirty panties and he always carried a pair on his route with him. For her eighteenth birthday Marshall gave LaKeisha five hundred dollars and she rewarded him with the sex he had spent nearly a year begging for. Afterwards Marshall strutted on his mail route and looked forward to his next sexual encounter with LaKeisha while he continued to collect her soiled panties. Marshall's wife finally found the panty collection and that, among other things, led to their separation.

Marshall liked to brag to LaKeisha about his sons, Leroy and David. When he told her they were going to the nearby community college she tracked them down and seduced them. They hooked up at that dance party held in the Duncan Hotel. LaKeisha had done her homework and knew they would be there. When she saw them, she walked right over and said, "Hi, your father is Marshall Ferguson right? Then I really need to talk to both of you outside for a minute." She ushered them to a secluded spot then said, "Let me get straight to the point. I live in Nelson Park and I been doing your daddy for over a year. Hey he's good...real good so I figure if he's that good, he can only make better...and I want to find out. I want to do both of you...NOW!"

Overwhelmed by her boldness the young men were putty in LaKeisha's hands. She had wanted these

two only because Marshall bragged about them as though they were Gods. They followed her to an empty apartment in Nelson Park and into their first freaky sexual experience. LaKeisha sucked them separately then both at the same time. She fucked Leroy while sucking David, then switched them around, finally ending up with Leroy's dick in her pussy and David's dick up her ass. She made it last as long as she could, being the meat in this sandwich was a dream come true. Drunk with lust and excitement she savored the feeling of two big hard dicks sliding in and out of her, one stroking her pussy and the other pounding her ass.

The three of them spent the rest of that night and early morning in that apartment. LaKeisha was in heaven. Both of Marshall's sons were well hung and could fuck faster and harder than Marshall. LaKeisha fucked them over and over, she sucked them, tittie fucked them, licked their bodies, and demanded to be the meat in the sandwich one more time before sending them home completely drained and exhausted.

Over the next few weeks she tried but could not get both of them together again because David had a girlfriend he was kind of serious about and quickly lost interest. Leroy however was just as horny as LaKeisha and the two of them have been fucking like rabbits ever since. Marshall didn't have a clue. Throughout all of this LaKeisha was still fucking him as much as ever.

While in beauty school, LaKeisha grew up and realized she was now on her own and needed to move out of her mother's apartment. To cover her back a sugar daddy was not enough, she needed regular legal access to Marshall's wallet and to accomplish that she decided to get pregnant. She told Marshall she ran out of birth

control pills and spaced it out. The pregnancy was an accident but she loved Marshall so much she couldn't bear to murder his child. If he didn't want to support the baby or see her again she would understand. Marshall ate this shit up and swore his love and devotion to LaKeisha and his unborn child.

But...from the first time he put his dick in her Leroy didn't miss a beat. He was fucking LaKeisha at least three times to Marshall's one and Leroy was the ONLY one fucking LaKeisha during her first two weeks off the pill...when she got pregnant. LaKeisha was a happy woman and she sang while she worked.

Chapter thirteen

Within ten months of the takeover, Tamika's Total Hair Care offered every service of cosmetology for women and men. From perms to pedicures, haircuts to shoe shines, Tamika's shop done it all and business was booming. Even Florence Johnson was impressed. Ruth Ann however was not. She took to calling me "The Cradle Robber" whenever she saw me in public. I was plenty tired of her shit so when she started demanding money and threatening jail again, I tried to shut her up by asking if she would give permission for Tamika and I to marry. Actually, Tamika was past nineteen and did not need parental permission. In spite of that however, Ruth Ann had the fucking nerve to demand ten thousand dollars for her permission anyway. That really pissed me off so I made Tamika the happiest girl on the planet. I purchased two round trip tickets, made reservations and we flew to Las Vegas for six days.

We vacationed, got married, yeah that's right! Got married at one of them Vegas Wedding Chapels then floated around on cloud nine. Tamika made some long distance phone calls and we returned to a large wedding

reception party at LaKeisha's apartment.

Shortly after we arrived, Ruth Ann stormed in and made her announcement, "Winston Littles, ah ain't got but one thang tuh say tuh you!" she began. "Ah ain't never in life goin tuh cept yo old black ass as no son-in-law of mines! And Miss Tamika Rochelle, ah's glad to be rid of yo smart-ass! You wanted dat old mutherfuckah now you gots him, so stay yo smart ass wit him and don't bes lookin to me fur shit!"

"Hey...Ruth Ann! Come on now," Wanda pleaded.

"Fuck you Wanda!" Ruth Ann snapped. "And fuck all da rest of ya'll dat thank dere's somethin heah tuh cellbrate. An old ass mutherfuckah robs da cradle, goes an marries a stupid young girl and you mutherfuckahs ret to party...huh?"

"Shut the fuck up Ruth Ann! Turn the music back up!" an unidentified voice called out.

"Ah don't needs dis shit!" Ruth Ann shot back. "And ah won't stand round heah and take it neither! Old mistah mutherfuckah and uppity Miss Tamika, y'all wallow round in one nuthers shit long as you wanna, just don't be branging none of it round to my doe!" With that Ruth Ann turned and started for the door, then stopped and said, "Come on Wanda...lets git da fuck outta heah!"

"Hell naw!" Wanda replied. "I came to party...ain't no way I'm gonna miss this...hee-hee-hee..." Wanda returned to the giggling fit she had been having since Tamika and I first walked in.

"Uh huh," Ruth Ann responded, "ah sees who MY friends really are...well awl ya'll can KISS MY BITCH ASS!" She slammed the door behind her causing some to

applaud and everyone to crack-up.

Despite Ruth Ann it was a great party. We showed the video of our wedding, cut our cake, danced, celebrated and had a good time. The number of people that had lost money betting I would never get married amused me. Winston Littles married? Sounded funny but here I was back at home in Nelson Park a newlywed. I had never seen Tamika so gracious, beautiful and proud. This girl had changed my thinking then my life. I'm twenty-two years older than she but our age difference is really not a factor. We share something very special and very precious. You know when you are truly in love and for me it was my first and only time. I've had many women of various descriptions but Tamika is the first and only woman I have ever really been in love with. It is only now that I really know and am comfortable with this. We partied until late in the night and got back to my apartment tired, but happy lovers, in love.

We awoke the very next morning and instinctively knew it was time to move. This apartment had been my bachelor pad for, well quite a few years. It could never be ours. We needed a brand new home to start our brand new life as Mr. and Mrs. Winston Littles.

My wife and I spent four days looking at apartments, compared notes then decided to go first class. We wanted it, we could afford it, and Tamika had certainly earned it. So we leased a luxury two-bedroom apartment in an expensive high-rise building near downtown called The Strathmore Towers. Our soundproof sixteenth floor apartment has central air conditioning, plush wall to wall carpeting, with marble tile kitchen, laundry room and baths. It has two huge

master bedrooms, each with a large bathroom and two walk-in closets. The apartment also includes two half baths, a den, a dining room and a sunken living room leading to a large balcony with a built in Jacuzzi and a stunning view of the city. We even have private underground parking and were bursting with excitement after signing the lease and getting our keys. Tamika immediately got busy selecting the perfect furnishing and decorations while I moved our personal stuff in.

I was back at Nelson Park, picking up the last of our things and waiting for Tamika's brother, Sam. He was gonna take my old apartment. The manager agreed to leave it in my name and look the other way long as the rent was paid on time. Sam was also taking over my car repair business. I sold him my tools, spare parts, customers and a couple of old cars. He had helped me out a few times and I had taught him a lot about cars over the years, so I gave Sam the apartment and sold him the business for almost nothing. Our deal was one hundred dollars a week for twenty weeks. I had to charge him something cause I didn't want to make a bad hustler out of him. I had faith in Sam and I was sure he would make something out of this little start. When a knock came at the door, I thought it was Sam and shouted, "Come on in it's open."

"So it is true...huh? Y'all's ass packin and runnin. Whut yuh runnin from old mutherfuckah? Yo conscience...huh? Or maybe Nelson Park ain't good nough no mo fur da uppity Miss Tamika...is dat it?" Ruth Ann fumed.

"Give it a rest why don't cha Ruth Ann," I replied.

"Oh yeah...hell yeah, dat fuckin shit's easy fo yo

old dog ass tuh say. Awl da fuck you ever dun is take from me and now you dun took my baby…and you wants me tuh bes happy and quiet bout it! Well fuck you old mistah muckerfuckah! Ah ain't happy and ah don't gives a fuck who knows it! Don't nobody gives a fuck bout Ruth Ann. Wit yo ass stealing Tamika, my welfare check dun got cut way da fuck back and ah ain't got her to help out round da house no mo…but do you gives a fuck? Hell naw…you ain't gave Ruth Ann shit…nuthin…not even da time of day…da least yo old broke ass coulda done was come round and give me sum dick once in a while," Ruth Ann wailed.

"What?" I questioned, hoping I heard wrong.

"Don't whut me old mutherfuckah!" she snapped. "You heared me. Course you been fuckin dat child so youse probably done forgot whut real woman pussay feels like…a good shot of some real pussay would fuck yo old ass head completely up!" Ruth Ann began to undress as she spoke.

"Ruth Ann!" I called out.

"I'm takin some of whut you owes me in dick!" she insisted.

"Ruth Ann don't do that put your clothes back on," I pleaded.

"WHUT! WHUT? You tryin tuh say you don't wants dis pussay?" Ruth Ann indignantly questioned.

"I'm saying you are drunk and I am a happily married man," I responded.

"Fuck you old mutherfuckah, fuck you in yo stuck up ass…you probably can't git it up no mo…dats whut it is…ain't it? Old ass mutherfuckah done gone and married a young ass child and can't git it up no mo! Well dat's all right baby dis here pussay will git it up…den

you can put it in dis booty where it's supposed to be anyhow...ain't it? You knows you supposed to be fuckin me Winston not dat child. You knows dat and you knows dis always been yo pussay...anytime you wanted sum. Me and you always could throw down...and we was real good...you knows dat...now come on...come on...give it to Ruth Ann! Come on goddamnit!" she demanded.

"Ruth Ann take yo drunk ass home!" I ordered.

"Ah ain't goin no fuckin place till ah gets some mo of dat dick," Ruth Ann insisted. "You needs to realize you dun fucked up and settled fo a dime when yo black ass coulda had a dollah! Now come on boy...give Ruth Ann dat purty black dick...don't makes me go off on yo ass!" Ruth Ann was now completely naked standing in the middle of my living room grinding her butt around and licking her own titties.

"Okay Ruth Ann," I agreed. "Once more for old times sake. Go spread that hot ass across my bed like you used to while I find some incense and put on some music."

"Now you talkin baby...now you talkin...shit dis booty ain't seen no real good dick in years!" Ruth Ann crowed then headed for my bedroom, switching and rubbing her ass all the way.

As soon as she was out of eyeshot, I grabbed the boxes I had packed and ran out the front door leaving it wide open. I hurried down the steps and out the entrance to the building. A crap game was going on in the courtyard so I asked, "Hey fellahs anybody want some hot pussy?"

"Hell yeah!" they all replied in unison.

"Apartment 3C, the front door is wide open and

the bitch is buck naked, laying on the bed jonesing for some dick!" I advised.

All five crapshooters, including seventy-four year old Amos, immediately rushed to Apartment 3C.

Chapter fourteen

In spite of the fact Tamika couldn't drive, we bought a brand new, four-door Mercedes Benz for her twentieth birthday. The dark blue Benz was our family flagship and we were very proud of it. Tamika's eyes would sparkle every time I drove up in our Benz to pick her up from work. I always got out and opened the door for her and she never failed to make a graceful entrance into the car. Life was good and we were happy. We ate in fine restaurants, enjoyed our luxury apartment, took short trips in our flagship and spent hours in each other's arms.

On the day they were hired Tamika required each of her beauty school graduates to train at least two apprentices in their specialty. By doing so she expanded the size and knowledge of her general staff while silently pushing her graduate staff to perform at a level worthy of admiration from their customers and especially from their apprentices. That high level of quality service paid off and about one year after she took over Flo's, Tamika opened a second hair salon on the eastside. Florence Johnson was named manager of the

Nelson Park salon and Darnell...rather Darlene was named manager of the new eastside salon. Darlene was proud, happy and put tremendous energy into running a first class salon. She was closing up the salon one evening when a persistent male customer would not go away. Without question Darnell was a good-looking woman and had gotten used to being one. He looked better and acted more like a lady than most women he passed on the street. This customer who begged, pleaded, then offered money, service and lifelong devotion was determined to fuck Darlene. When she grew tired of him Darlene backed the customer into a corner, raised her dress, dropped her panties and showed the man her dick. The poor man was speechless. He bolted for the door, stumbling and bumping into the furniture. He hit the street in a dead run and crashed full speed into a parked car, knocking his big ass to the ground and sending his false teeth sliding several feet into the street.

Darlene walked out of the salon and locked the door as the stunned customer was struggling to his feet. "Your next appointment is on the sixteenth at three thirty, be on time!" she snapped, then got into her little red sports car and drove away, narrowly missing the denture still lying in the street.

Exactly six months after the second salon opened, Tamika opened a third near downtown. Although all of Tamika's hair salons had an unusually large number of male customers, the new mid-town salon was expected to have an even larger percentage. LaKeisha, the lady with the excellent barbering skills was named manager of the mid-town salon and she took it to heart. LaKeisha had given birth to little Marshall then joined a health

club. She always had big titties but the rest of her body filled out during the pregnancy and LaKeisha was determined to stay sexy and shapely. Her tight barber uniform was more than a little bit revealing and LaKeisha proudly strutted her stuff. She had a great personality and set the example for her employees by fussing over each customer. Mid-town was an instant success.

For my birthday Tamika bought me a small fishing boat and a lot of gear. Rods, reels, lures...stuff like that. She even leased storage at the lake so I wouldn't have to tow the thing. I was never much of a fisherman but since my baby bought it for me; I play with the shit every now and then. Sometimes I even catch a fish. Hell, one day I took the boat all the way out to the middle of the lake.

When I returned home that day Tamika was in our den that also served as her office. There was a small stack of House and Home magazines growing daily on the table and her desk was covered with plans for her fourth salon. I gave her a big hug and kiss. Looking deep into those adoring eyes does wonders for the ego and sometimes I wonder if my old heart can stand feeling this good much longer. As it was though, I took a shower then returned to the den. The phone rang just as I was going for another one of Tamika's sweet, sweet kisses and damnit she answered the thing.

"Hello...hi Lester...what? Oh no! Damn I'm sorry to hear that! How's he doing? Uh-huh...is Drey there? Uh huh...tell you what Lester, I want you to call me when he is out of recovery and into a room...and can talk...okay? Meanwhile I'll send a plant or something to cheer him up...huh? Oh...I'm sure...yeah he'll be

okay…sure…bye Lester. Darnell's been in a car wreck," Tamika informed me. "It's serious but he's getting patched up now and they are pretty sure he'll be okay."

"You wanna go to the hospital?" I asked.

"No…not until Lester calls and tells me he is in a room and can talk. I refuse to go stand around a cold hospital hallway and wring my hands," Tamika replied.

She seemed very calm, not too worried or bothered, so we ate dinner, watched a little television and had sex before drifting off to sleep.

Two days later Tamika dressed in her professional best and we went to the hospital. When we entered Darnell's room I was amazed. He had tubes running out of him and a lot of bandages on but the son-of-a-bitch still looked like a woman. When he saw Tamika, Darnell started whimpering,

"Oh Tamika, I'm so glad to see you…I been so scared…it all happened so fast…I don't know what happened. I just don't know what happened?"

Tamika smiled as she leaned over Darnell and in a soft firm voice said, "I'll tell you what happened Darnell. You been stealing from me, that's what happened. I audited your shop and discovered the shorts. You were stealing and we both know it, so don't try and deny it. Your bank deposits didn't match your customer ticket count on several days. I even have you on videotape doing the daily report, separating your take from the day's receipts and putting money into your bra. Never forget this experience Darnell! No one steals from me without paying dearly. I had one of "your" employees loosen a coupling in the brake line of your car so your brake fluid squirted out every time you put on your brakes. Eventually you ran out of brake

fluid...and boom...here you are. You were lucky this time Darnell and you only get one more chance. Pay back what you stole and don't ever steal from me again. It really is as simple as that! Now hurry up and get outta here, I need Darlene back on the job." She kissed Darnell lightly on the lips then abruptly left the room.

Darnell looked at me with wide amazed eyes; I shrugged my shoulders and followed Tamika out the door. Tamika never spoke a word about what she had said to Darnell and I certainly never brought it up. But you can believe I discovered a newfound respect for my wife.

The fourth salon was the most upscale and opened almost eight months after the third salon. It was located in the north end of town. Avery got the job as manager and took Sheila with him. None other than the strict Florence Johnson had groomed Avery for this job. She had made him an assistant manager then rode him constantly, hoping to get him promoted out of her salon. She did not like Avery's skinny white grinning ass and her efforts paid off. Florence was happy to see him and a few others go. Tamika had used the Nelson Park Salon as a training camp for new and management employees. After the north salon opened, Avery, Sheila and the remaining trainees left. Sister Florence was happy and the Nelson Park salon had a "going away" party for them...the day after they left. Avery and his crew performed their jobs well and the forth salon sprang to life. In about three months the north salon was operating smoothly and successfully.

Following this Tamika decided the time had come for us to buy a house. She had pretty much settled on what she wanted with the help of that growing stack of

House and Home magazines. I was easy to please, so we went house hunting. By the time Tamika found the perfect house they were all starting to look alike to me. But she knew exactly what she wanted and 7602 Crestwood Boulevard was it. Deep in an affluent suburb called Ridgewood Estates our house sat on five acres of trees, gardens and rolling green lawn. It was a two-story English Tudor style mansion, with a huge foyer, several fireplaces, five bedrooms, seven baths, a formal dining room, a comfortable den and a big mahogany paneled library, which became Tamika's office. The house also had a large recreation room containing a pool table, bar, piano and a giant swimming pool. The pool was half indoors and half out. During the colder months the pool service put glass enclosures around the outside part. We also had a workout room with a lot of exercise equipment, a sauna, Jacuzzi and several of the bathrooms had whirlpool tubs. Across from the pool there was a rather large party house with a loft and above the four-car garage was a two-bedroom apartment.

We moved in shortly after closing the sale but since we loved our Strathmore Tower apartment we kept it too, staying there when Tamika had early morning business in town. Rhonda Hutchinson, a short fat girl from Nelson Park became our housekeeper. She was an excellent cook and a jolly person whom life had not treated very well. For her this was a dream job and she moved into the luxury apartment above the garage. In truth, I think Rhonda was more impressed with her apartment than we were with our house. She was very professional and did not meddle or pry. For the most part Rhonda paid Tamika and me little attention and

happily went about her work, cooking, keeping the house spotless and managing the estate. For several days I walked through the house and around the beautiful grounds in awe. I had never in life even expected to visit such a house but here I was living in grand luxury. Tamika and I acted like little kids at times, running naked across the lawns, having sex in the gazebos, wading in the small stream that led to a reflecting pool and dancing through the fountain.

Sam came to visit and was impressed beyond words. We slapped five so much my hand was burning and I was relieved when I noticed Sam and Rhonda making eyes at each other. I excused myself and left them in the kitchen, then later learned that Rhonda was standing at the sink when Sam walked up behind her. He put his arms around her and started feeling on her big titties.

Rhonda sighed then turned around and said, "Look Sam I'm gonna be straight with you. I love to get down, I really do, but I don't get many chances out here so don't go starting something unless you are willing to finish it."

Sam grinned and placed Rhonda's hand against his hard-on. "Does that feel like I mean business?" he asked.

Rhonda giggled and insisted they go to her apartment although Sam wanted to get it on right there. Rhonda would have no part of fucking in her employer's kitchen or anywhere else on the estate except her apartment.

Through the intercom Rhonda asked for a short break and I quickly gave her the rest of the day off. The minute they entered her apartment, Sam continued his

tittie attack while a happy Rhonda undressed both of them then clamped her mouth on Sam's dick and sucked him. It had been a long time since Rhonda had made love so she was very eager, hot and wet. She loved sucking dick and took her time, gorging herself, much to Sam's delight. Finally she rolled over and drew her legs up tight to her shoulders. Sam was excited, he slid his hard dick into her tight, wet pussy and fucked her vigorously, amazed at how good her pussy really was. He was even more amazed at how comfortable and wonderful her ample body felt to him. Early the next morning Tamika and I giggled as we watched Sam's car disappear down the driveway. Later we were not surprised or offended when Sam visited Rhonda, but not us.

For Tamika's birthday that year I had a large oil painting done from her little photograph of Benny Monroe. She cried when she saw it and we hung the painting over the fireplace in her office. Occasionally Tamika would get high and talk to the painting as if her father were alive. She really loved him and she loved that painting. Even Rhonda began speaking to Benny when she came in to clean the office and strangely enough most of Tamika's salon managers nodded or spoke to Benny when they came on business. Needless to say I was quite pleased with myself. Having that painting done was probably the second best thing I had ever done for my wonderful little wife.

Ruth Ann was quite another story. Tamika offered to buy her a house but she refused. Tamika offered to lease Ruth Ann a nice luxury apartment and she refused that too. Ruth Ann was only interested in cash. Truth is, Ruth Ann had a cocaine habit and she

refused to leave her suppliers in Nelson Park. She told Tamika point blank that she had lived in Nelson Park all of her adult life and knew every swinging dick and fonky hoe there. She was comfortable, happy and satisfied so unless you had some money for her, leave her the fuck alone.

It was several months before Ruth Ann got around to visiting our new home. Sam brought her out one day and Ruth Ann did not have a good word to say about anything. She got out of Sam's car swearing we done got in way over our heads. When she stepped onto the marble floor of our foyer, she asked what the fuck we needed with this big ass barn. As she entered the living room, Ruth Ann accused us of trying to live like white folks. Her tour of the house stopped dead still in Tamika's office. When she stepped into that room the first thing she saw was the oil painting of Benny Monroe and Ruth Ann lost it. "AW NAW! Where da fuck did you git a picture of dat dirty, low life, two timin mutherfuckah?" she wailed.

"He's my daddy, ain't he?" Tamika asked.

"He's a no good sorry mutherfuckah, dat's who he is goddamnit!" Ruth Ann insisted.

"But he IS my daddy, right?" Tamika demanded.

Ruth Ann whirled around. "You da spittin image of his smart ass. Yeah! He yo goddamn daddy alright and ah don't has to stand round heah and look at neither one of youse. Sam get me da fuck outta heah! Ah don't see no big ass pictures of Ruth Ann hanging no fuckin place!"

"Mama chill out…please!" Tamika pleaded.

"Fuck you Tamika Rochelle! You wants me to stay heah a minute longer den burn dat fuckin picture rat

now!" Ruth Ann ordered.

"I ain't burning my daddy's painting!" Tamika firmly replied.

"Den fuck you! Fuck yo daddy! And fuck dat dirty old mutherfuckah yous married too! Sam...SAM...take me back tuh Nelson Park, where da sho nuff folks live...ah've had bout much of dese uppity mutherfuckahs as a body can stand...and da longest day ah live, ah don't never needs tuh see nother picture of Benny's black ass! Ah don't needs dis shit...just insult da fuck outta Ruth Ann...uppity little smart-ass wench! Dis big ass yard looks like a fuckin cemetery..." Ruth Ann babbled all the way back to Sam's car. She got in, slammed the door and rode off, never to return to our home again.

Chapter fifteen

As the year neared the end Tamika and Rhonda were excited and busily planning the first big party to be held in our splendid home. It was going to be a Christmas party for Tamika's employees and as their planning picked up, so did the errands. Now several months back we bought a brand new, big ass Buick station wagon for Rhonda to use, so she could run them damn errands as far as I was concerned. I went fishing, visited friends and generally made myself scarce for awhile.

I was in our downtown apartment, admiring the view and thinking about Tamika. She was an amazing person. I felt very lucky to be the one she chose to share her life with and I thanked the good Lord for giving her to me. Without her persistence and determination we would have never hooked up to begin with. My life would not have changed and none of this would have happened. The lady is smart. She has vision and instinctively knows what buttons to push. Damn I really love that girl. She has so many good qualities it seems a shame that she doesn't want to have a child to pass those

good qualities on to. But on the other hand that child could take after Ruth Ann. The world would never forgive Tamika for putting another one of them hellcats on earth, so maybe once again Tamika knows what she is doing. The phone rang and I answered it. "Hello?"

"Hi Sweetheart," Tamika sang into the phone.

"Hey baby, I was just thinking about how much I love you," I replied.

"Rhonda and I have finished the party plans, so you can stop hiding and come home," Tamika informed me.

"Hee-hee...what makes you think I been hiding?" I responded.

"Winston...ha-ha, I love you so much...don't even try it. You been scarce as hens teeth the last four days cause you didn't want to run errands...ha-ha-ha," Tamika giggled then continued. "We are done and Rhonda is tying up the loose ends, so you can come back home now I miss you."

"Tell you what, since Rhonda is running errands she's probably got to come downtown anyway, so why don't you have her drop you here and we'll spend the night," I suggested.

"I'd love to sweetheart but Rhonda has left already," Tamika advised.

"In that case I'll be home in a few minutes," I promised.

"I can't wait to get my arms around you, I'm gonna melt my body and pour it all over you," Tamika purred.

"Shit, I just left and I wish that Benz had wings so it could fly," I responded.

"Be careful and don't speed. I'm going to take a

bath and dream about my wonderful husband," Tamika whispered in a sexy voice.

"Lord, lord...I'm outta here, see you in a few," I repeated.

"Okay...bye sweetheart," she replied.

"Bye baby."

Tamika and Rhonda laid out a fabulous party. It was staged in our rec room and in the party house on the other side of the patio. The pool service removed the glass enclosures around the outside of the pool and installed one big electric heater on each side of the patio. The warm air blowing across offset the winter chill, so our guests were comfortable inside or out. Tamika hired a popular local rhythm and blues band plus "The Divine Miss Gina Devine" with her co-stars Georgette and Toni to entertain.

Along with a formally dressed expanded house staff we had two parking valets and each of our guests and their party was assigned at least one formally dressed personal waiter or waitress. A professional chef and his staff oversaw the buffets and I have never seen so much food. All kinds of hot and cold hors d'oeuvres, a whole pig, steak, prime rib, fish, shrimp and chicken cooked four or five different ways. All kinds of fruits, salads, dips, greens, potatoes, peas, tomatoes, corn, breads, pies, cakes, at least ten different kinds of ice cream, puddings and gelatins. If you can think of it, it was there somewhere. To compliment that we had two full service bars set up complete with professional bartenders.

Another formally dressed waiter converted the loft of our party house into a drug den. On the coffee table he laid out a thin two-foot long line of snow-white

cocaine. Then using a little machine he rolled about one hundred marijuana joints. He put a small pipe stuffed with a big hunk of hashish, three short lines of cocaine and several joints on small silver trays and placed them around the loft. He put the remaining joints into a large silver bowl and put it on a side table. The waiter then filled a large hand carved pipe with a mixture of marijuana, hashish and cocaine. The pipe held close to half an ounce of weed and had several tubes attached to it so more than one person could smoke from it at the same time. Finally the waiter looked around and was satisfied. The drug den was ready and he rewarded himself by sampling the cocaine.

Tamika and Rhonda hustled about checking details and decorations, while I chased off a waiter and waitress who had been assigned to help me dress and get ready.

The first guest began arriving early in the evening. Among them were Sister Florence Johnson and her husband Elder Cecil L. Johnson, Sr. Florence was clearly uncomfortable as she placed her gift for the company exchange under the tree and plucked her bonus envelope off it. She munched a few peanuts and accepted a small glass of punch from her personal waiter then asked Tamika for a few words in private.

When they emerged from Tamika's office, Elder Johnson was seated at a table happily laying claim to a huge plate of food. He smacked his lips and took his time while the agitated and impatient Florence glared at him. He finally wiped his mouth and leaned back, only to reach over, grab a big dish of peach cobbler and direct his waiter to bury it with ice cream. When he finished, Florence was tapping her foot and burning with anger

but the Elder kept his seat and sucked his teeth.

"Cecil", Florence hissed, "we do have other obligations tonight!"

"I know, I know, just hold on a minute," the Elder replied.

The waiter was honored to serve The Johnson's. His grandmother worshipped at Gladstone Baptist and she always spoke of Elder Cecil Johnson as a true living saint. A few minutes later the waiter appeared with a large box which he insisted on carrying to the Elder's car.

"God bless you son, God bless you," Elder Johnson cooed.

"What's that?" Florence snapped.

"Just a little something to snack on later," Elder Johnson chuckled. The box contained a whole slab of ribs, two steaks, two large cuts of prime rib and a whole fried chicken, along with six large servings of several different kinds of food plus one whole peach cobbler. Elder Johnson smiled big as he offered "God bless you and Merry Christmas to all" while keeping a close eye on the waiter and his precious cargo as they made their way out.

The party picked up almost as quickly as the Johnson's left. Everybody was dressed to the nines and looking good. Food, drink and drugs were consumed, gifts and hugs were exchanged, bonuses were removed from the tree and the party was in full swing when Tamika stepped to the microphone to officially welcome our guest. "I wanna know...are you having a good time?" she asked.

The audience cheered in response.

"Thank you and thank you all for coming," she

continued. "Winston and I are really happy you are here. We want you to get comfortable, relax and really enjoy yourself. Eat, drink and be merry! Later, if you need to crash you are welcome, or if you must go home and are in no condition, we have limos standing by. This is your Christmas party and it doesn't end until after breakfast! Now...to make sure you all have a real good time...we have a special surprise I know you will enjoy! A wedding will be held here tonight!"

Some people gasped, causing Tamika's smile to broaden, the secret had been kept.

"Right here and right now..." she continued, "Drey Dickerson and Darlene Freeman are going to exchange marriage vows. Our party house has been converted into a chapel just for this occasion and the betrothed request the pleasure of your company at their special ceremony. So...if you will all just step across the patio, the wedding will begin as soon as everyone is seated. Once again thank you for coming to your party and MERRY CHRISTMAS...EVERYBODY! Maestro..."

The band kicked off a wedding march and everybody headed for the party house giggling or whispering to each other.

Once we were all assembled, suffered through two solos and some kind of poetry reading, a short fat uncomfortable looking preacher entered the room and stepped to the altar. Drey followed him dressed in a sharp black tuxedo. As soon as the men were in place, the band jumped into a lively version of "Here Comes the Bride" and Darnell...rather Darlene cascaded down the steps from the loft. Darlene had gained some weight since getting out of the hospital and I'll be damned if she didn't look good, real good. Smooth round hips, that

well-known bubble butt straining against the fabric that covered it, small waist and I don't know whether it was padding, hormone shots or just natural but she had some damn decent titties too. She wore a tight fitting, full length, shimmering pale yellow gown with a matching tiara and veil covering her face, while her hair flowed softly to her shoulders. A man that didn't know better could easily get a major hard-on just watching Darlene walk. She moved purposely and sensuously toward the altar, while Wilona sat staring at her only son in disbelief and Lester grinned from ear to ear.

They couldn't get married legally but they publicly pledged to love, honor, respect and cherish each other till death they do part. They exchanged rings and finally heard the minister say, "I now pronounce you life partners. Young man, you may salute your bride." With nervous shaky fingers Drey raised his bride's veil then kissed her right on the lips. It was a wet, passionate loving kiss that grew intense and lasted way too long.

The sweaty preacher tried to look the other way while the audience hooted and cheered. Finally the preacher announced to the audience, "Ladies and Gentleman...I now present...Mr. and Mrs. Drey Dickerson." Again the audience cheered then the piano player begin playing and singing their special song, the first song they had danced to, "I Found a Love by Wilson Picket." The newlyweds danced lovingly at the altar staring into the others eyes. Drey was still nervous and sweating but he was a happy man. He looked deep into Darlene's eyes and saw only true love. Overcome by it all Darlene began to cry as Drey held her close massaging her back until the song ended. All while

Tamika, LaKeisha and a few other women cried, Wilona stared and Lester grinned.

When the song ended the newlyweds were ushered to the head of a receiving line, and most of the guests lined up to wish them well. Now quite frankly, I was down right amazed at the number of men that kissed the bride. I'll admit she looks damn good! Hum…damn good and a half. BUT…she's still a man.

When my turn came I told them I admired their courage and wished them well while stuffing ten one hundred-dollar bills into Drey's hand as a wedding present. I ignored his and Darlene's thanks or objections or whatever it was they said and went on about my business. Actually, I wanted to watch that sweaty preacher eat. He started eating when he came through the door and stopped only to perform the ceremony. Last I saw him he was about to attack a whole lobster. It was live before the ceremony and you guessed it while he was doing his duty, the lobster was a-boiling. While looking for ole greedy preach I noticed Wilona start for the receiving line but she stopped short, hesitated then went up the steps to the drug den instead.

Following the reception line a three-tier wedding cake was cut, toasts were made and a professional photographer took formal photos before making his exit. The photographer was sharing a complimentary limo with the little fat preacher who was already waiting on board with his to go box of goodies. The photographer was also given a to go box on his way out as this was a no holds barred Christmas party…preachers and cameras were not allowed!

The band had been kicking up the tempo and finally jumped off into, "Ain't No Stopping Us Now" and

the party was on again. Eating, drinking, dancing and laughter everywhere. About forty minutes later, just as darkness set in I went to a store room in the party house to switch on the far back patio lights and there was Drey and Darlene. Darlene was on her knees with a mouth full of Drey's big dick. She stared up into her new husband's eyes.

Drey was about five inches taller than Darlene he was slim, dark and had curly hair. "I love you baby" he whispered in a husky voice. "I love yo pretty ass so fucking much I can't stand it and I mean that shit! Goddamn...I really mean it Darlene, I love you baby. You mine...all mine! We done took our vows before the whole goddamn world...we official and everything...you all mine now pretty baby! Aw yeah...all mine...uh-huh...worship this dick pretty baby...it's all yours...every fucking bit of it belongs only to yo fine ass...Mrs. Dickerson! Ah yeah...suck it...suck it pretty wife."

Darlene sucked in nearly all of Drey's big black meat and was clawing at his bare ass when Drey pulled her to her feet and covered her mouth with a sloppy kiss. They clutched and grabbed at each other, obviously unaware of my presence.

"Oh I'm so happy...God...I love you so much my beautiful husband...I want you, I want you now!" Darlene gasped as she turned and leaned over a table.

Drey lifted her dress exposing Darlene's soft round ass. She was wearing only a leather jock strap underneath. Drey spit in his hand then rubbed it on his dick. I was real interested now cause Drey had a dick like a barnyard animal. It was thick, hard as nails and must have been twelve inches long. I couldn't believe he

was gonna put all that dick into Darlene, but he did. With one slow stroke he pushed about a third of it in. Darlene pooched up his butt and with only a few more strokes Drey's giant dick disappeared completely. With his dick buried deep in Darlene's naked ass, Drey reached out and pulled his new bride to him. He tilted her chin up and they exchanged several wet sloppy kisses while slowly grinding.

"Oh Drey...Drey...hurt me sugar...hurt me with that big dick! Oh God...it's so good...yes...yes...oh God I love it. I really fucking love it! Oh hurt me...hurt me!" Darlene wailed.

Drey pushed Darlene forward, grabbed her by the hips and started long stroking that big meat in and out of her. When his hips started smacking hard against Darlene's butt it became just a little too damn much for me so I flipped the outside light switches and eased out of the room.

On my way back to the rec room I began to feel sorry for Wilona, both her son and companion where involved with men so I decided to check on her and went up to the drug den. She was sitting in a high bar chair with a drink in one hand and a joint in the other. It was not without reason that Tamika assigned two very attractive and very horny young waiters to Wilona, and they were on the job. One was sitting on the floor massaging her feet, while the other was playing with her titties, stealing kisses and challenging her to hit the big pipe. Wilona was obviously enjoying herself so I set off to find Tamika.

As I walked across the patio I saw LaKeisha floating in the pool. She was completely naked, comfortably lounging on a large inflatable swan,

pushing grapes into her pussy and ordering her waiter to lick them out. I continued into the rec room where several guest in various states of undress danced, lounged or hung around the bar. The Barnett's were sitting on a love seat grinning. Avery lay at their feet wearing a collar and holding a leash. On a table in front of them was a twelve-inch line of cocaine and I couldn't imagine what the hell they were up to, so I nodded and kept going.

Tamika was in the foyer saying goodnight to some departing guests so I joined her. A few minutes later we said goodnight to the chef and most of the professional staff, leaving two bartenders, our expanded house staff and the personal wait staff to look after our remaining guests. Tamika was very happy but tired so we went up to our bedroom to sit on the balcony and view the wild party going on below. And it was wild. The Divine Miss Gina Devine and her cohorts were shaking booty all over the place while the band played a furious funky rhythm. Aaron was behind the bar on his knees sucking one of the bartenders who leaned on the bar and acted as though nothing was happening. Naomi, Tamika's older sister had joined LaKeisha in the pool. Naomi was also naked and making her waiter lick grapes out of her pussy. Dot was standing close to the pool loudly assuring Sam she could suck his dick and balls at the same time. Rhonda walked past and accidentally on purpose bumped a fully dressed, perfectly made-up Dot into the pool. Rhonda kept going to a waitress station out in the yard and bent over to refill her tray. Soaked and mad as hell Dot climbed out of the water marched across the yard and kicked Rhonda squarely in her ass. Rhonda turned around and

grabbed Dot by the neck, yanking her feet off the ground and holding her in the air.

"Now you listen to me you little worthless piece of black trash!" Rhonda roared. "If you ever touch Sam or raise your bony leg to kick me again, I'm gonna rip it off and shove it so far down your damn throat your toes will be sticking out your pussy. Do you understand me gal? Do you?"

Dot blinked her wide frighten eyes and croaked her understanding as best she could before Rhonda slammed her to the ground and stormed off. Dot immediately leapt to her feet and raced to the foyer, demanding her car from the valet. She was headed home to take her hurt and anger out on her sometime boyfriend, but her personal waiter first begged her to stay then begged her for a blowjob. Dot granted both his requests.

A few minutes later, Drey and Darlene rushed across the patio and on to the foyer. They hustled into their limo and off to parts unknown to begin their honeymoon.

About this time the party turned from wild into an orgy to behold. On stage the girl singer leaned over a high stool and crooned a sexy song, while behind her, Gina Devine raised both their mini-skirts, pushed his dick into her pussy then eagerly began fucking her. The singer didn't miss a note while Gina fucked and his fellow female impersonator Toni unbuttoned the front of his dress and began jacking off. He then approached Gina from behind and started rubbing his dick up and down the crack of his ass.

The music stopped in mid-song then recorded music was switched on because a completely naked

Naomi walked onto the stage. She stopped in front of the guitar player, bent over, pushed his guitar away, opened his pants, pulled his dick out, stroked it then started sucking. The drummer dropped his sticks, got behind her, pulled out his dick and shoved it into Naomi's pussy. Meanwhile Georgette a male impersonator who kept most people guessing had seized a waitress; undressed her on stage and was very busy giving the happy woman a head to toe tongue massage. Toni danced around the stage. He wore a long one piece tight fitting gold dress that buttoned down the front. Two buttons at crotch level were open and Toni's hard dick hung through. It was a strange sight to be sure, because in drag, Toni was one truly fine, high yellah bitch. She had long brown hair and filled that dress to the breaking point. But now with that hard dick hanging through the front of her dress, you got the full impact of the word "queer." He alternated between dancing and standing at the edge of the stage jacking off. Soon as he got his dick real hard, he'd start dancing again. He danced around and through the hot heady sex happening on stage. He sprinkled cocaine on the head of his dick and Gina Devine stopped fucking the girl singer long enough to sniff it off before sucking the head of Toni's dick for a brief moment before Toni fluttered away into the strong embrace of the piano player. He stood behind Toni and slowly slid his hands from below her thighs all the way up to her silicone titties then back to her dick. He kissed her neck, jacked her off and came in his pants.

This party was hot...RED HOT! The whole place sizzled everywhere you looked nasty exciting sex was going on. Even Rhonda gave in to the heat and was

humping Sam on a chase lounge. They lay on their sides, Rhonda was tittie feeding Sam and hunching her pussy up and down his dick in fast short strokes. Suddenly she threw her head back and screamed, then covered Sam's mouth with hers and wildly cranked her pussy on Sam's hard happy dick.

Two lesbian waitresses were giving LaKeisha a body to body peanut butter and whipped cream massage. All three were naked and all three had stacked firm young bodies. One waitress covered herself with peanut butter, the other with whipped cream. LaKeisha lay on a rubber mat close to the pool. The waitresses approached her from opposite ends, and slowly kissed and slithered their way to the other end. Pausing to kiss and tongue each other when passing. When LaKeisha was well lathered, those four hands, four titties, four lips, two tongues and two sweet pussies drove her hot sexy ass to another dimension. Seductively, passionately those three beautiful young bodies slithered together in a wild orgy of touch. Tamika smiled, this was a special surprise gift she had arranged for LaKeisha and she happily watched her best friend wiggle and cry out in heated ecstasy.

On the far side of the patio, the Barnett's and their slave had shared several lines of cocaine and were totally fucked up. The three of them were naked and excited by what they were seeing. Avery lay at Sheila's feet wearing a collar and holding a leash while Woodrow reclined on a redwood deck chair grinning and occasionally stroking his dick. Sheila hooked the leash to Avery's collar and paraded him around the pool on all fours. Wagging his butt Avery stopped to sniff every available asshole, dick and pussy on the way, but

when he sniffed his Massa's dick, he opened his mouth and quickly sucked most of it deep into his throat. He moaned and gurgled when he felt his Massa's heavy hand massage his head. For Avery, there was nothing in life better than this. He gorged himself, doing his best at giving his Massa a superior, wet, tight-mouthed blowjob. He happily sucked dick until his Misses yanked his leash. Just as Avery's mouth released Woodrow's dick, Sheila placed one knee on each side of Woodrow and sat down on him. She leaned back and rubbed Woodrow's dick back and forth against her clit.

Sheila was in heaven, fucking in public was just one more fantasy she had longed to fulfill and to make it all a whole lot sweeter, for the first time in her life she really had something special to show off. She had a husband with a big dick and she had a young white boy...her very own personal love slave. Nothing could stop Sheila from making the most of this opportunity and really show off. After tonight everybody was going to know she can and does handle both these dicks. In fact she needs as least two good dicks regularly, she was a woman's, woman! A bad bitch with a real man AND a real love slave. Sheila was tripping, her pussy was dripping wet and she felt a giant rush when Woodrow pushed his hard dick into her. She leaned back to get it in deep and for a few moments watched Woodrow's big dick slid in and out. Then she leaned forward, brushed her nipples across Woodrow's tongue, put her hands on top of the deck chair and started fucking. She pumped hard, riding Woodrow's big meat all the way in on every stroke. Woodrow pumped just as hard and they fucked furiously for a few minutes. Juice poured from Sheila's pussy and her big titties violently thrashed about.

Suddenly she yanked the leash snapping orders to her slave boy. Then leaning over a little more, putting her hands on Woodrow's chest, she humped her ass up higher. Avery quickly got behind her, worked his dick deep into her asshole then reached around and grabbed two handfuls of tittie. The three of them were good together; quite obviously they had done this shit before. At first both men remained completely still while Sheila pumped back and forth fucking both of them. Then Sheila held still while Massa Woodrow and slave Avery got a back and forth rhythm going and fucked Misses Sheila vigorously for quite a few minutes before all three of them got into a hot, funky, deep grinding routine that created some serious wailing and moaning.

Meanwhile Nuggy had his two waitresses sucking his dick. First one...then the other, then both. He stood up and the girls started with his feet and kissed their way to his dick. One sucked his dick, while the other licked his balls and the crack of his ass. Nuggy attempted to squat to let the waitress tongue his asshole, but it was too good. He lost his balance and toppled over. Laughing he ordered them to sit on him, one on his face and one on his dick. Nuggy was having big fun as was Aaron and Lester who were rubbing butts and dancing naked on the pool table.

When the music slowed, Aaron sat down on the table then laid back raised his legs and started playing with his plentiful dick. Lester watched then stood over Aaron and pushed his legs back against his shoulders, allowing Aaron to suck his own dick. Lester mostly used his mouth and ass for sex. As Wilona could attest, Lester didn't get hard often and he rarely fucked anyone, but watching Aaron suck his own dick was too much even

for Lester. He hungrily studied Aaron licking, sucking and really enjoying his big meat.

Lester began to grunt as his dick got hard, really hard. He looked at Aaron's asshole puckering at him and grinned. Lester held Aaron legs back with one hand and stroked his own rare hard-on with the other, then squatted and rubbed his dick across Aaron's asshole. Aaron's soft moans sent a chill through Lester, exciting him as he gently pushed the head of his now throbbing hard-on into Aaron's ass. It was hot and tight but Aaron knew how to use his sphincter to massage Lester's dick. So with almost no resistance Aaron's asshole quickly accepted the aching dick pushing into it. Lester screamed with delight and lowered himself, forcing his dick even deeper into this delicious willing ass. They were both freaking, Lester couldn't take him eyes off Aaron, the harder he fucked the deeper Aaron's dick went into his own mouth.

Aaron winked his eye at Lester. He loved sucking his own dick and it was even better with Lester watching him and pumping hard dick up his ass. Lester was deep grinding into Aaron's ass while Aaron was eagerly drinking his own cum when Wilona came down the steps from the drug den.

Escorted by her waiters, Wilona was highly aroused and feeling no pain. While getting high she had watched much of the wild sexual action taking place below from the loft. She watched and thought about sex...fucking. All her life she thought about fucking a lot but seldom got to. When she did it just never seemed to be enough. Wilona was raised with strict Christian values and had never really expected a good sex life. After many disappointments she mostly suppressed her

desires. She knew Lester was a little freaky, but he was a good provider and a good companion. He wasn't violent and sex was not a big issue in Wilona's life. But tonight…after watching her only son marry a man, then actually seeing Lester seriously play with other men and all these other people going at each other. Wilona decided to get her share too.

If Wilona had a fantasy it had to be handsome, horny young boys and at this party she had two of them. Tamika gave them to her. They were her property for the entire evening and that fact had already sunk in.

She paused at the bottom of the steps then ordered her waiters to carry her to the same altar her son had gotten married at. The young men spread several pillows before the altar then picked up Wilona carried her to it and gently placed her on the pillows. At her command they quickly stripped and stood naked before her. She had them pose, parade, turn slowly around, bend over, stoke their dicks and dance.

Finally Wilona allowed her young men to undress her. She was excited and breathing hard. Never had she had sex with a man so much younger than her and never had she had sex with two men at the same time. She took her time kissing both her young lovers, sucking their tongues and moaning. She trembled with anticipation as she commanded their tongues and lips to explore her ample yet shapely body.

One of Wilona's studs was nineteen and the other had just turned twenty-one. They devoured her sex-starved body like two hungry wolves. Wilona roared to the first of many new highs as the younger stud sucked, licked and made sweet love to both of her generous titties. While the older one went straight to the pussy,

found the correct spot and done some serious tongue work. Wilona wailed and violently shook her head. In but a few minutes she climaxed with a powerful rush. It was her first real unassisted climax and it only fueled her lust.

When the young men backed off she ordered them to stand before her so she could study their hard young dicks. Wilona had never sucked a dick though she had long wanted to. For some reason it had just never happened but it was going to happen tonight. She sat up, reached out and took a dick in each hand. Thrilled by their hard yet soft feel, she gently stroked them. For several moments Wilona admired and played with these dicks before she lightly rubbed the youngest boy's dick across her closed lips. Too hot, too real and too far to turn back Wilona parted her lips, then slowly but with growing excitement sucked that hard young dick into her anxious mouth. The taste and feel of it ripped through her body with such an intense thrill she immediately wanted more, she wanted all of it. Wilona gorged and gagged herself trying to suck all of it, stopping only to suck the other boy with equal hunger and enthusiasm.

Taking her time she intensely sucked first one then the other before again lying back on the pillows. The younger boy straddled her face offering his hard-on to Wilona's eager mouth, while the older stud returned his tongue to her wet, hot, trembling pussy. Wilona moaned, clutched at her young lovers, sucked dick and moved in rhythm with the wonderful tongue licking her clit. When the older stud's man-sized dick slipped into Wilona's tight pussy she freaked. Gasping so hard she swallowed nearly all of the dick she was sucking. It

slipped deep into her throat and she liked it.

A tear trickled from Wilona's eye, having a young hard dick down her throat while another plunged deeper and deeper into her wet starving pussy was driving the poor old girl mad. She gave herself with wild joyous abandon. Losing count as grippingly intense climaxes sent waves of powerful explosive thrills and spasms through her body. Both her mouth and pussy were dripping as those hard young dicks pumped in and out. The freak in Wilona was being set free and she would leave this party a different woman.

When the young man she was sucking felt his cum build he instinctively tried to pull his dick out of Wilona's mouth but she grabbed his ass dug her fingernails in and to the young man's absolute delight, forced him to cum in her throat. The older stud soon pumped hot cum deep into Wilona's pussy but their party was far from over.

The waiters moved Wilona to a guest bedroom, stocked it with food, booze and drugs then eagerly gave their dicks and hearts to her. Making up for lost time, Wilona continued happily sucking, fucking and playing with her two young lovers until late the next morning. In point of fact, Wilona now had no intention of letting these sweet young dicks go. She promised them all the pussy they could handle then made plans and immediate arrangements to meet and fuck again and again. Without apology to Lester she continued to see both young men separately and together for many years following our little party.

Back out by the pool the band was back at work and playing another old favorite when a food fight broke out then ended with damn near everybody in the

swimming pool. Some were dressed, some not. Laughing, howling and shouting at each other, they climbed out of the pool toweled off then resumed eating, drinking, getting high and fucking up a storm. Tamika and I were feeling no pain as we stood up and hugged each other.

"You know something Winston? Since the day I knew you would be mine I have not even thought about having sex with someone else," Tamika offered.

"Something on your mind now?" I asked.

"Yeah," she replied, "I want Keisha to deliver what she promised several years ago."

"What's that?" I questioned.

"I want her to lick me and I want you to fuck me while she does it. Would that be okay?" Tamika asked.

"Fine with me," I agreed.

"You sure sweetheart?" she questioned. "Don't say yes just to please me. It will never happen if it's not okay with you!"

"Not to worry baby, you deserve a reward and I have no problem with it," I assured her.

"Good!" Tamika declared. "I can't wait. I'm ready to get this done!"

"Hum…been thinking on this huh?" I teased.

"Of course!" Tamika grinned, winked her eye then stepped back into our bedroom and began removing her clothes.

Before leaving the balcony, I took one more look around at the action below then summoned LaKeisha to our bedroom. I had just undressed and joined Tamika on our king-sized bed when LaKeisha sprang through our bedroom door wet from a quick shower and wearing only a towel. Her firm shapely body was way more than

an eye full and she quickly agreed to Tamika's request, as long as she was also allowed to suck my dick too.

"I been wanting to taste this old meat for years," LaKeisha giggled. "Can I fuck him too?"

"Only if he wants you to!" Tamika replied.

"Not so fast!" I put in. "Let's get on with the original plan first."

I lay on my back and Tamika scrambled on top of me. With her back to me, she sat across my stomach and ordered LaKeisha to suck my dick. LaKeisha didn't hold back, she sucked my dick like she truly loved it and my Johnson was hard as nails in too short a time.

Tamika worked my hard dick into her then lay back in my arms with LaKeisha nested between our legs. With one hand she massaged my balls while her tongue flicked across Tamika's clit. Tamika sucked in her breath when LaKeisha's hot mouth covered her pussy and her tongue began attacking, teasing then softly licking her clit while I slowly pumped my dick in and out of her. LaKeisha pulled my dick out of Tamika, stroked it then repeatedly smacked it against my baby's pussy. She pushed it between Tamika's pussy lips and began licking the head of my dick and Tamika's clit at the same time. Following that she vigorously sucked my throbbing meat before pushing it back into Tamika's hot pussy.

"Fuck her Mister Winston!" LaKeisha gushed. "Fuck this child...come on...do it baby...you sweet fine sexy old dog! Fuck my sweet little cousin...aw yeah! She loves yo black ass Mister Winston...stroke that sweet pussy...ooo give her some dick baby...do it Mister Winston."

LaKeisha clamped her mouth onto Tamika's

pussy and for several precious moments the three of us became one giant sex organ. Heaving, grinding and thrusting together in perfect harmony until Tamika came. I was almost jealous because she came with such wild force, bucking and screaming. For a few moments she went totally fucking nuts. She damn near pulled LaKeisha's hair out and I was fighting to hold on to her when suddenly she went totally rigid and stopped breathing.

After what seemed an eternity, she cried out, took several short breaths, sighed repeatedly, pumped her pussy up and down my dick then slid off and snuggled close against me breathing hard and totally exhausted. "I love you Winston, oh...my sweet beautiful Winston...I truly love you more than you will ever know! This was so fucking great! I mean just really fucking great. This whole night has been great! Totally fucking great! Wow...damn...I'm drained but I'm happy...so happy...and so in love. I love you Winston Littles," Tamika purred.

"What about me...hell I done all the work!" LaKeisha put in.

Tamika and I laughed then kissed a meaningful passionate kiss that lingered and lingered while LaKeisha went back to sucking my dick and well shit it was all feeling mighty good. Tamika smiled when she saw how hard I was.

"Okay Keisha...you can fuck my baby...but you better make it good, make him cum hard, then get your ass outta my bedroom...ha-ha," Tamika instructed with a chuckle.

LaKeisha giggled, crawled on top of me, grabbed my dick and slid it into her hot wet pussy. Now I mean

to tell you I love Tamika and nothing will ever challenge that, but praise the good lord LaKeisha got some of the best pussy I have ever had. Somehow it just seemed to wrap itself around my dick, so instinctively I grabbed her hips and pumped all my dick into that hot talented pussy.

"Aw yeah!" LaKeisha cried out, "we gonna do some sho nuff fuckin huh? Aw yeah…aw yeah…gimme that old dick…give it to meee! Oooo shit…Mister Winston…oooo…oooo! Fuck you Mister Winston…fuck you! Oooo!"

Tamika cradled my head and smiled at me while LaKeisha leaned forward, arched her back then humped her pussy until all of my dick was inside her. She flattened her titties against my chest and we done some delicious hard wet fucking for what seemed a good long while.

"Goddamn!" LaKeisha shouted. "You hangin ain't you Mister Winston…Oooo…shit! You hangin baby…umm…fuck you! Oooo fuck you! Shit! Shit! Now I got to use my best stuff on yo ole ass."

She rose up, sat erect, played with her titties then slowly began to ride up and down my dick. Her wonderful pussy was grabbing even sucking my dick as she rode faster, getting wetter, big titties bouncing. I rose in time with her sensuous rhythm…but too much…oh yeah…too fucking much! I grabbed those beautiful tan thighs and hung on until cum literally exploded from my dick. I was suspended in complete fucking ecstasy, wrapped in the arms of my true love, cumming hard into her best friend. LaKeisha screamed then rode me hard and fast for a few precious moments before her own excitement boiled over into a powerful climax that

caused her to plunge into my arms, shrieking and gasping.

The after glow was beautiful. Both ladies clung to me as for several moments time disappeared. I stroked their soft supple bodies while both of these beautiful ladies covered my mouth and ears with wet passionate kisses. Naked female flesh completely covered me.

LaKeisha's pussy squeezed and tugged at my dick while she sighed deeply. She kissed me passionately on the lips, sighed again, touched her fingers to my lips then rolled off on my other side, saying to Tamika, "Girl! This old muther gonna kill yo ass. Do he fuck that long all the time? Goddamn my shit is still jumping and carrying on. No wonder I don't see much of you since you been married...shit you must be wore out most of the time. Damn! I know I can hang...but I wasn't expecting to meet up with this old dick from hell...he don't even stop to rest or nothing...it's a wonder you ain't dead Tamika! You good ole Mister Winston...I give you that...you good but a lady gotta be ready for yo ass!"

Tamika and I were cracking up. "Shut up Keisha and relax," Tamika responded.

"I'll relax for a few minutes, hell I ain't got enough strength to leave now anyway...but if that thing starts getting hard again...I'm outta here strength or no damn strength," LaKeisha promised.

Lying comfortably between these two fine sexy young women was hog fucking heaven. I drifted off to sleep and awoke awhile later to find both girls playing with my dick. More than cousins, Tamika and LaKeisha were best friends, they grew up together, were always there for each other and somehow this act of sharing me

meant a great deal to both of them. They whispered looked into each other's eyes then kissed each other long and hard. Tamika poured a small quantity of syrup on my dick and guided it to LaKeisha's mouth. For several minutes she stroked her cousin's hair while LaKeisha lovingly sucked my dick, then Tamika poured more syrup and joined in. My dick slid smoothly in and out of their mouths and between their sexy lips. Several times they shared a kiss with each other and the head of my dick. It was glorious!

They spent considerable time loving my most grateful dick, before they poured syrup on their titties and gave me a tittie fucking I will never forget. Good...Oh lord...who can describe this? Those four beautiful titties thrilled the shit out of me. First one set...then the other...on my dick...in my mouth...one set...then the other...Then BOTH! My dick has never been so happy!

Finally Tamika kissed LaKeisha on the lips. "The next time I kiss those lips, I want to taste my man's cum!" she whispered, then melted into my arms and covered my mouth with a wet passionate no let up kiss. LaKeisha's hot mouth sucked my dick in and I gasped. Both women were using their mouths to the maximum on me. I fucking floated...this shit was so good I didn't want it to ever stop. But in spite of myself I felt my cum start to build. My ladies sensed this and stepped up their attack, provoking me to a climax so powerful I still can feel it. LaKeisha went for it all, sucking and swallowing until I was dry.

After we settled down the ladies went to shower. Before joining them I stepped out onto the balcony expecting to see a complete mess. To my great surprise

the place was spotless. Rhonda had rounded up her staff, supervised the cleaning of the party area and preparation for breakfast while we and our guests slept. Several folks were still asleep, but Rhonda and the staff stood by to serve them when they awoke.

Tamika and I were very impressed. We enjoyed a late breakfast with our remaining guests and surprised Ronda by announcing that she was being rewarded with a five-day, all expenses paid vacation for two at a resort in Jamaica. To no ones surprise she immediately chose Sam to go with her. As our guests slowly departed Tamika gave each of them a "care package" containing food, booze and drugs. She paid the staff and the entertainers double their expected salary then insisted they split the remaining food, booze and drugs among themselves. There was still plenty of everything and the employee's care packages were even bigger than those our guests had received.

Tamika, Rhonda and I stood at the front door as the guests, entertainers and finally the wait staff left. I understood them hugging and kissing Tamika and Rhonda but I was annoyed when they hugged or kissed me. I was really annoyed when a male tried to hug or kiss me. And damn if several of them didn't try. I even had to quickly turn my head cause that damn freaky ass Toni tried to stick his nasty tongue right into my mouth.

Later that day the pool service re-installed the glass enclosures, cleaned the pool and removed the heaters. Tamika and I were very happy and very, very satisfied. We had given a party! A true party, a real, wild wonderful party few would ever forget.

Chapter sixteen

Life was good at 7602 Crestwood Boulevard, real good. For Christmas we traded in our Mercedes. It had been a great car and we loved it but it had a few years on it and Tamika recently discovered that ours wasn't the top model. She made it crystal clear to me and to the Mercedes dealer that I was to drive nothing less than the top-of-the-line complete with all available options. We paid the difference in cash and rolled out of there in the absolute best Mercedes had to offer.

Tamika really wanted to get a Rolls Royce, but I had to remind her that some of her shops were in neighborhoods that I was not going to drive a Rolls through, let alone stop long enough to let her out or pick her up. Hell I can't even think Rolls Royce, not where I come from. Some damn fool just lean on it and I got to shoot him. No question about it! A fool's life is cheap…you can make a new baby any damn time you want, but if you get even one old Rolls Royce in your whole lousy life you damn lucky. Naw, wasn't time for no Rolls just yet, but hell this new Benz couldn't be all that far behind a Rolls, this mo-chine is a real trip. I can't

even describe it to you. I guess you might say it's kinda like driving the executive suite, if you know what I mean. We rolled out of the dealership with nine miles on our new flagship and by the time I rolled it into the garage on Crestwood it had one hundred and four miles. You might say we cruised the long way home and somewhere along the way while playing with the many gadgets, I called the car "Bubba". Tamika loved it. So...we officially named our big silver Mercedes Benz "Bubba."

In the early spring, Tamika and I took a long leisurely five-week vacation to Hawaii. It is a special and beautiful place especially to people in love. We learned a lot, enjoyed new experiences, relaxed and had a great time. On the long flight home we began talking about real estate investments. Tamika wanted to diversify her holdings and real estate seemed to be the best bet. She didn't open any more hair salons but did buy a beauty supply store. It was a good economic move. By doing so she lowered the cost of supplies to her salons, sold to the general public and established a long-standing family business that provided employment for her sisters Naomi and Jewel and her brother Nuggy.

In late-summer Tamika and I were having a late breakfast by the pool and discussing real estate ventures when a nervous Rhonda approached and announced that the police were at the door wanting to speak to Tamika. The police had in fact followed Rhonda to the pool area and stepped past her.

"Tamika Rochelle Littles?" one of the policemen asked.

"Yes," Tamika replied.

"Mrs. Littles, we have a warrant and are here to

place you under arrest for pandering, solicitation and operating houses of prostitution," the police announced.

Despite my protest and objections the police read Tamika her rights and put handcuffs on my precious baby. I hurriedly called our lawyers and followed the police car to the station.

Apparently, the police had raided three of Tamika's Hair Salons and found a live, functioning Glory Hole Club in each one. From the start a small separate room had been set aside in each salon and the Glory Hole Club had been a viable part of each operation, except Nelson Park where it operated off and on because of Florence Johnson's strenuous objections.

It was Saturday and the lawyers informed me that bail could not be set until Tamika was arraigned and that wasn't likely to happen until Monday. I had a horrible weekend. It hurt terribly to visit my baby through a dirty glass jail partition and I was determined to get her out there fast. Finally on Monday the lawyers got her out. She was scared, shaken and starving because she refused to eat jail food, so I rushed her right home for some of Rhonda's good home cooking and a nice hot bath.

The north, eastside and midtown salons had been closed and the managers, Avery, LaKeisha and Darlene had been arrested but the dick suckers who were working at the time of the raids escaped.

Tamika had done her homework and carefully designed each operation to include a small storeroom with outside access on the second floor above each salon. A small light on the outside of the building was lit up when the GHC was open. The unmarked door to the small room housing the GHC in each salon was inside

the men's restroom. Just like the outside light, the inside door was controlled from the suck booth by an electronic switch and locked when the GHC was closed. Once inside that door the customer faced two booths from which to choose. Each had a slide bolt on the inside that showed vacant or occupied on the outside. Upon finding a vacant booth the customer stepped inside and locked the door with the slide bolt. Inside the booth was a dim light in the ceiling, on the back wall was a small step block for short guys, two grips for hanging on and a small rectangular slot above the glory hole which was at crotch level. A small sign at eye level explained the procedure and cost. The customer slid his money through the rectangular slot and the door covering the glory hole opened. The customer guided his dick through the hole and got a great blowjob. Simple, efficient and anonymous. There was no visible entrance into the inside of the suck booths. Entrance could not be gained through the salon or on any side of the walls enclosing the room. The dick suckers entered and left thorough the ceiling using ladders they pulled up into the storeroom when they left. Each Glory Hole Club had a hinged ceiling. Even the molding rose with the ceiling and fit so well, that with the side bolts in place they were virtually undetectable.

The three salons were raided simultaneously and at each one the police wasted valuable time trying to find an entrance to the interior of the suck booths. Finally they called for axes and sledgehammers so they could smash through the reinforced wall housing the money slot and glory hole. At each location the booth wall was smashed but the small interior room which had no windows or door was empty. The police were

stunned and spent considerable time searching before finally discovering the ceiling exits. This was discovered only because the fleeing dick suckers at one location did not take time to put their slide bolts in place. It had been a smooth operation. Tamika rented the Glory Hole Clubs and only she knew to whom. The salon managers, the customers nor the police had any real idea as to just exactly who was behind those walls sucking dicks and the raids were essentially a big fat failure.

Because the interior of the Glory Hole Clubs could not be accessed from inside any of the salons and since the police failed to photograph or document the evidence before smashing the walls, the salon managers were quickly released without charges. All three salons re-opened the next day but the prosecution focused on Tamika. She was the owner of the salons. They had scared customers and police informants willing and ready to testify plus Florence Johnson was their key witness. The only thing missing was the actual dick suckers, but with Florence to provide some inside information, the prosecution was talking tough.

Tamika fired Florence Johnson and sent me to the Nelson Park salon to collect her keys and clean out anything Flo left behind. As luck would have it, on my way home from the salon I passed The Gladstone Street Missionary Baptist Church. A sign out front advertised some kind of video competition program the next Sunday. I immediately parked the Mercedes, went inside and inquired about the program. Mistaking me for a church member and parent, the junior minister cheerfully explained that a film production company had provided basic instruction then loaned the church five professional video cameras. All the interested

church youth were assembled into five teams and each team had written and produced their own film with the theme being, "Glorifying the Lord". The time limit for each film was twelve minutes and first prize included a trophy and savings bond for each team member. This coming Sunday, right after morning services was the big moment, showing and judging time.

When the gabby junior minister told me the video cassettes had been turned in and were under his care until showing, I walked him outside. A three hundred dollar contribution to wherever he saw fit, helped the junior minister decide to accept my daughter's brief little video as a special entry. I made a fast round trip, delivered the video and watched the junior minister mark Florence Johnson's infamous tape a special entry then lock it away with the others.

On the following Sunday afternoon, to my great satisfaction, Sister Florence eagerly sucked and fucked two young studs on the big screen while over three hundred stunned church-goers watched in shocked silence. Her show only ran for a few minutes before nervous fumbling hands stopped the video, but Florence was immediately and totally ruined.

At first Tamika was shocked by what I had done and was sad for Florence, but before long we were giggling in each others arms and spent the night laughing, hugging and generally celebrating Florence Johnson's fall from grace.

As the trial grew closer Tamika grew more tense and quiet. She was a having a hard time with all of this. The whole atmosphere of defense planning, court appearances, continuances and legal back and forth was wearing her down. Not to mention that the IRS was

waiting in the wings, ready to file tax evasion and under reporting of income charges the minute she is convicted. A couple of weeks before the trial was to begin she went to our downtown apartment. She told me she wanted to be alone to review her defense strategy and mentally prepare herself. Very reluctantly I left her there and drove back to our suburban home. I couldn't relax or sleep. Other than her short stay in jail we had never spent the night apart from each other since before we were married.

Shortly after midnight Tamika called, she was upset and didn't want to be alone. Within minutes I rolled the Mercedes into the Strathmore and rushed to our apartment. Tamika met me at the door and we talked until sunrise. Ordinarily I didn't presume to meddle in Tamika's business. She was very capable and I respected that but on this night she told me the burden was too great. She did not have any feel for the legal affairs she now faced and was feeling insecure. She needed me. That was all I needed to hear. I promised to relieve her burden, made sweet passionate love to my wife...gently rocked her to sleep then went to work.

My first stop was our lawyer's office and my only question was, "How much money would it take to get this thrown out...period?" The lawyers were coy and kept hedging, referring over and over to the prosecutions strong case. But the way I saw it all they had was Florence Johnson's big mouth and a few fools, most of which the police paid to stick their dicks through a blind wall.

I got tired of listening to the lawyers babble and set off to find Florence Johnson. I knew she would be mad as a hornet but to my way of thinking this was the

perfect time to buy her off and without Florence the case gets a whole lot weaker. So I drove back to the Strathmore and called the Johnson residence. To my great surprise a terse sounding woman informed me that Florence Johnson no longer resides in that house and her present whereabouts were unknown.

I didn't have the phone numbers of the real busy-bodies in Nelson Park, so bright and early the next morning I parked the Mercedes between the dumpster and the wall then for the first time in many moons walked back into the Nelson Park projects. Funny how once you are gone you have trouble believing you really used to live there. Nonetheless, in about two hours I had the low down on Florence. Turns out she ran from the church minutes after the video was shown, packed a bag and disappeared. So they say she went down south to stay with her sister. Sadly, Elder Cecil was removed from the church on a stretcher and spent six days in the hospital. On the fourth day of his hospital stay however, Elder Cecil filed for a divorce. Word has it, the process servers spent days snooping all around the Nelson Park neighborhood but they could not locate Florence to hand her the papers.

Without any real insight or serious thought about what I was actually doing, I had struck a deathblow to Florence Johnson and scored a three-base hit for my wife. My little indiscretion with that video had knocked the pompous balls right off of this case and I went straight back to them garbage breath lawyers. If the process servers for the divorce court could not find Florence neither could the same monkeys from the prosecutor's office. "So how much to get this shit thrown out?" I questioned. Apparently, this bit of new

information inspired those legal vultures to begin seeing things my way. They promised to began negotiations and get back to me in two days.

And get back to me they did, with a figure so goddamn high I hung up the phone and went straight to their office. We were being flat out ripped off and I knew it. You see, without ole long gone Florence the case didn't amount to shit. Tamika could cop out to a lesser charge and only get a fine or probation. But the thing was…she couldn't afford a conviction of any kind because the IRS was honed in and ready to pounce the minute the word guilty rose from the courtroom. I know them gangsters with degrees on both sides got together and estimated Tamika's net worth, split it among them, then pushed like hell to get every penny of it. By bankrupting Tamika, our lawyers, the judge and the prosecutors would fatten their pockets and put a friendly fucking on the IRS. But, to my pleasant surprise, Tamika was a lot sharper than those turkeys gave her credit for and their best guess at her net worth wasn't even close. But they had us by the short hairs and they knew it.

First they demanded three hundred and fifty thousand dollars. Then after a whole lot of straight-out nasty, down dirty and low-life bartering we finally agreed on two hundred and twenty-five thousand dollars. From that the lawyers would pay themselves and who ever else needed paying. All charges will be dropped and Tamika walks away a free woman. I used my best stuff to get to two hundred and twenty-five thousand dollars and they would not go below that no matter how bad or good I talked. I tried every trick I know, even made real nasty explicit sexual remarks

about their mamas and daughters. First I endeared myself to them, then I tried to make them hate me, finally I got sick of them so I broke it off and settled. I walked out of the lawyer's office with a very expensive deal pending Tamika's approval. No way in hell was I happy about it but it was the best I could do.

I went home, set down with Tamika, held both her hands and completely explained everything I had done, where the case stood and the deal I had made including how much it cost. For a moment I was startled. With my own eyes I actually saw relief flood all through Tamika. She began to shake and tightly gripped my hands. For the first time in many weeks her eyes began to sparkle. She cried, then laughed, then danced around the room, then hugged me so tight I nearly lost my breath, then she danced around the room again. Money seriously didn't mean a damn thing. Tamika's only goal was to be out of this shit, done with it and not go to jail. The money didn't matter, being free to be herself mattered and she was happy. More than happy, she was excited and thrilled. Suddenly she was in my arms, squeezing, hugging, kissing, crying some more, my sweet baby was all over me.

Truly Tamika was a happy woman and I had more than half expected she would, at the very least, be upset by the amount of money the settlement was going to cost. I was pleased that she was so happy but I was still pissed off at them thieving legal vultures in their tacky look-a-like over-priced suits. I quickly mellowed out though and lost my thoughts to Tamika's sweet and oh so eager lovemaking. Her joy was special and we knew we had reached a new level in the depth of our feelings for each other. I pray everyone, except those

lawyers, can know this feeling and share a love this intense. We spent the rest of that day and night as we so often did before this legal shit started…hugging, playing and enjoying each other while passionately celebrating our love.

The following day Tamika and I went to the lawyer's office and paid fifty thousand dollars to finalize the deal. We agreed to pay the remaining one hundred seventy-five thousand dollars in sixty days. They offered more time or installment payments with interest but we weren't interested. We agreed to pay in full within sixty days, end of conversation.

Tamika and I had already talked about this the day before. If we were going to pay our way out then we should do it quick and final. We were not going to up the ante by paying interest and we would be up shit creek if Florence Johnson should suddenly reappear. We wanted it fast and final with all charges dropped in such a way they cannot be re-filed.

The lawyers accepted our position then informed us that all legal liens or holds placed against Tamika's assets by this case would be removed in a few days. Then they offered to expedite any paperwork should the sale of any assets be deemed necessary. "SHOULD the sale of any assets be necessary?" Now I have to tell you I do hate all shithead lawyers but Tamika was squeezing my hand so I knew she wanted me to be cool. I bit my lip until I got to the door, then just before leaving I smiled a big ole toothy smile and asked, "Can you guys handle one more question?"

"Certainly Mister Littles, what's your question?" the chief dirt ball responded.

"How do you guys operate so well in daylight?" I

asked still smiling.

The lawyers were not amused but I was quite pleased with myself as we left.

We had a few days to wait before the assets were clear and needed time to think so I took Tamika fishing. We would talk for a spell then Tamika would make notes on a large yellow pad of paper. The new car, the trip to Hawaii plus paying legal fees had done a serious number on the savings in ole promise number three. To raise the needed money it was necessary to sell at least two, maybe three salons, so we decided to sell everything. All four salons, the Beauty Supply store and the house on Crestwood would go. We both felt it was time to seek a new direction so we seized this opportunity, agreeing to seek and explore new worlds. By day's end I hadn't done any fishing but we both enjoyed being on the lake and came back for the next three days in a row.

We whiled away four pleasant days floating on the river. I had become a much better skipper than a fisherman and cruised down river, dropping anchor off and on at a nice shady spot then throwing a line into the water. Tamika's eyes were sparkling. She spent most of her time writing notes on her yellow pads and gazing into the distance. Once we had broadly discussed ideas, possibilities and a general overview, her mind was off and running and she didn't need to talk very much. I understood this...in fact it was just one more thing I loved about my wife. We could be together for hours and not talk.

Tamika loved detailed plans and smiled while working out her liquidation guidelines. She calculated the worth then assigned estimated value, potential

buyers and target sale dates to each business, the house and furniture. Occasionally she made notes about new ideas or fresh challenges. I smiled at her thinking only of the present and how much I enjoyed being on the lake with her. Every now and then I would actually catch a fish but I had to throw them back right away. When I caught the first one, a little silver looking fish with purple stripes on it, Tamika thought it was cute. She named it "Poncho" then decided to keep it as a pet, planning to buy a fish tank and other junk for it, so back the others go right away.

During our third day on the water in mid-afternoon, I had dropped anchor and was busy trying to catch another fish. Tamika was deep into writing and thinking when another small boat came down the lake. The boat passed at considerable distance with a man and a woman in it. I waved just as I did at all passing boats and otherwise paid little attention until someone shouted, "Hey Winton? Winton Littles ain't dat you?"

I looked up and waved again as the boat turned around then eased up next to ours. Sonny and Velma Jean Davis were grinning at me from the other boat.

Sonny and Velma both had to be at least fifteen years older than me. Velma Jean used to live in Nelson Park. She was a fat, ugly, disagreeable bitch then and she is even fatter and uglier now. Sonny used to hang around Nelson Park all the time when he was dating Velma Jean. I used to work on Sonny's old Cadillacs. He never took care of his car and would buy one shitty old Cadillac after another, dog em out, then pay me to patch them up. I made plenty money off of Sonny and was sorry to see him finally marry Velma Jean. When she moved away so did Sonny's business.

Sonny was kind of a silly acting dude that was always trying to impress everyone. He wanted you to think he was a big shot and had a lot of expensive stuff. I've even known Sonny to go out and rent a car just to impress someone. Guess he was a good mate for Velma Jean because she was a true know-it-all and took great pleasure in correcting everyone about anything. I hadn't seen them in many years and had not wanted to see them. Matter of fact, I wasn't real thrilled with seeing them now.

"Ah thought dat was you Winton Littles," Sonny hollered. "How da heck you bin doin man? Ah ain't seen you in ah don't even know how long."

"Ay Sonny...Velma," I replied.

"Ah heard you done went and got married tuh a...uh...uh..." Sonny stammered.

"A CHILD!" Velma Jean snapped.

"Shut up Velma Jean," Sonny shot back.

"Well you heard wrong on that score," I responded. "I happen to have gotten married to this mature outstanding young lady right here and her name is Tamika."

"Pleases to meet cha, please to me cha," Sonny replied too eagerly.

"High you doin Tamika?" Velma put in. "Ah didn't means no harm nor sass, ah's jis tellin yous what folks was sayin."

Tamika nodded her head then looked at me, I could tell she really wanted to laugh in their face.

"Well ya'll certainly makes a fine lookin couple," Sonny grinned. "Yas suh a fine lookin couple. Has da little wife got you goin to chuch now Winton?"

"Going to church?" I asked.

"Now Sonny, you know long as we been knowin Winton Littles, he ain't never had no religion about em. But ah knows his wife go to chuch, don't cha honey?" Velma Jean asked.

"No, as a matter of fact I don't," Tamika replied.

"What? Lawd! Now don't you mess round and let ole Winton Littles makes you lose yo soul honey," Velma Jean lectured.

Tamika smiled then leaned forward slightly and replied, "To be quite honest Velma, Winston doesn't MAKE me do anything and I don't MAKE him do anything."

"Hum…well somebody ought tuh MAKE ya'll go tuh chuch," Velma Jean shot back. "What ya'll need is uh good chuch home, dat's what you need. See you don't haves to go ever Sundee, you jis pay yo tithes and go ever so often. Everbody needs a chuch home…why don't ya'll come on and go tuh chuch wit us dis Sundee. We gos up heah tuh Calvary Baptist, ya'll know where tis up dere. Doctuh Witherspoon's chuch, yuh know. Have ya'll heard Doctuh Witherspoon preach, honey let me tell you! Dat man truly gots tuh bes nointed cause he sho-ley can preach, you know whut I mean honey. Ya'll needs tuh come on and go wit us, yuh sho do."

"Alright, alright Velma Jean!" Sonny pleaded.

"You jis hush Sonny!" Velma Jean ordered.

Again Tamika leaned forward and spoke, "Thanks a lot Velma for the invitation but Winston and I are obligated this Sunday. If we decide to accept your invitation in the future I will give you a call and we will go as your guests."

"Yeah dat's a wunderful idee!" Velma Jean happily agreed. "Ya'll do dat, ya'll do it, ah'm gonna

write muh number down right heah. Ah'm gonna write it down and ah'm gonna give it to yuh and you keep it and you call me. You call me real soon cause ya'll just gonna have such a wunderful time. Ya'll jis gonna enjoy yo self so much cause let me tell you Doctuh Witherspoon, lawd dat man can preach, yes he can! Thank you Jesus! YES HE CAN! Yes he can...ya'll come on and go wit us nah...you jis gonna have a wunderful time, wunderful!"

"Alright Velma Jean, alright," Sonny pleaded again.

"Jis hand em dis, jis hand dis over dere to em Sonny, dat's what you do, hand it to em!" Velma Jean instructed.

Sonny was ogling Tamika, he handed me the slip of paper but continued to eye Tamika while asking, "Any fish bitin round here Winton?"

"Oh...some are some ain't Sonny," I replied.

"Aw come on man, don't bes tryin to fool me now, how many yuh done caught?" he asked.

"Hum...I don't know...probably six or seven," I responded.

"Humph...six or seven huh? What yuh fishin wit? Where yo bait?" Sonny questioned.

"Right here," I answered with growing annoyance.

"What is zat man? Dat ain't no bait! You needs worms! You ain't got no bait!" Sonny declared.

"I don't care nothing about fooling around with worms or live bait, I use this little plastic junk I got in the bait shop," I advised.

"No wunder you ain't catchin nuthin, where yo fish at?" Sonny asked.

"What fish?" I questioned.

"Da ones you dun caught lemme see em," he grinned.

"Ah...I ain't got em...I threw em back," I honestly replied.

"Threw em back? Ever one of em?" Sonny questioned with great suspicion.

"Yeah...every one of em...cept one Tamika got at home in a tank," I snapped.

"Man...? What kinda weird fishin you call yoself doin Winton? Ah doan member you even knowin how tuh fish in da furst place," Sonny chuckled.

"Well what difference does it make Sonny...long as I'm enjoying myself!" I growled.

Tamika stood up. "I feel like going for a swim," she announced then slipped out of her blouse, smiled and said, "Come on Velma swim with me you'll have such a wunderful time." With that she stepped from her shorts and for a brief moment stood completely nude and ran her fingers through her long straight hair. Tamika was not the prettiest girl in the world but over the last few years as she had grown into a woman her body had filled out and she was very well developed. She had large round perky titties, a smooth flat stomach, a small waist, a large firm round butt, beautiful legs and her skin was soft and smooth without a scar or blemish of any kind. She was completely delicious, a shapely, well groomed, soft brown woman with class. She winked at me then dived into the water.

"Let's go Sonny!" Velma Jean snapped.

Sonny was staring at the spot where Tamika entered the water. He grinned at me saying, "You got a whole lot of woman dere boy...hey hey hey..."

"Let's go Sonny!" Velma Jean again ordered.

"How long ya'll been married?" Sonny asked still grinning.

"SONNY! I SAID LET'S GO!" Velma Jean roared as Tamika surfaced then began swimming back to our boat.

"Ah'll see you later Winton," Sonny shouted as he started his engine and headed his boat down stream, rounding the bend then quickly disappearing from view. After I helped Tamika back into our boat we laughed and giggled for sometime then snuggled into each other's arms and for the first time made love in our boat. Making love on the lake spoiled both of us and we found a whole new use for our boat.

Chapter seventeen

A*bout ten days following* that $50,000 down payment the lawyers notified us that all assets were clear and Tamika sprang into action. She and Rhonda planned an informal dinner party for Tamika's salon managers and key employees and the invitations went out. Tamika saw these people as being her children, she had raised them and at this party they were going to graduate and step out on their own.

After a delicious dinner, Tamika announced the status of her legal case. She did not say so but implied that she had a large fine to pay then announced her intention to completely sell-off her assets. Everyone was being put on their own as Tamika was refocusing her business efforts in a different direction. She went on to state the invited guests, especially her managers, had first shot at buying the business establishments and within a few moments all the salons and the beauty supply business were spoken for.

It was a relaxed, fun party and once it moved out by the pool, each graduate was required to put on a

transparent cap and gown ordered especially for this party. Following that, a professional photographer took several individual portraits and the official class photo. This after all was a graduation party. Finally Tamika had each employee come forward one at a time and receive his or her diploma. The diploma was a personal letter from Tamika. The letters were beautifully handwritten on a parchment scroll and tied with gold braid. Tamika had taken considerable time with each one. To some she provided direction and to others encouragement. She seemed to know just exactly what each really needed to hear. Like royalty she stood on a platform beside a small table on the far side of the pool. To receive their diploma, each person was required to walk the complete length of the pool wearing their see through cap and gown, while the others cheered, whistled and hooted at them and the band played "Pomp and Circumstance."

Some party guests chose to completely undress before putting on the transparent cap and gown. LaKeisha not only undressed, she tightly cinched her gown on both sides making it skin tight and caused the room to sizzle on her graduation walk. Not to be out done, Jewel, Tamika's little sister, who was not so little anymore, took all her clothes off and tied her gown loosely around her neck and let it flow behind her as she gracefully paraded down the length of the pool. The girl had a dynamite body, she knew it, was proud of it and it showed. All eyes followed Jewel as she seductively slithered up and back raising everyone's temperature.

When the last diploma had been awarded, Tamika introduced me as not only the most important element of her life but as her key to life itself. I stepped forward and drew Tamika into my arms kissing her

with a long wet passionate kiss. The band kicked off one of them good old slow songs and we began dancing. In love and proud to show it, we were dancing so seductively I began to lose myself to the moment. Then for some reason our guests realized that Tamika and I were the only ones formally dressed. Without warning they attacked, pushed us to the ground, ripped off our clothes then threw us into the pool. To their dismay we continued slow dancing and kissing in the pool for a few moments before inviting everyone in for a game of water volleyball.

After a great time in the pool, we ushered our guests into warm robes and fresh drinks then on to our den. The band played several good oldies, ending with "auld Lang sine" as tears, hugs and kisses flowed freely while our guests and our friends said their good-byes and slowly began to make their way home. It had been a great party and I was especially proud of Tamika. All of her children had graduated with honors.

Within a week the money started rolling in. The Nelson Park salon was sold to Aaron. He had developed a large following of loyal customers and apparently had some well off contacts within his gay world. He quickly produced the full price in cash. Avery visited his natural parents and received a large sum of money for his promise not to visit again for several years or until he changed his lifestyle. The Barnett's got a credit union loan for the remainder of the selling price and in partnership with their slave bought the north salon. A group consisting of Drey, Darlene, Lester and Wilona bought the eastside salon. They got a small business loan and paid the remainder in cash. LaKeisha bought midtown for cash and a bank loan she forced Marshall

Ferguson to co-sign. Naomi, Sam, Nuggy and Jewel bought the beauty supply store for considerably less than the asking price, but they paid in cash and Tamika would not have sold it to anyone else.

About a year ago the Strathmore apartment building had been sold and was now being converted into condominiums. Because the house on Crestwood sold quickly and produced a larger than expected profit, we took advantage of being established lease holders and bought our apartment complete with our private two-car underground garage in the Strathmore. We bought at a below market price and paid in full. Tamika re-done the condo with our favorite pieces then sold the rest to a furniture dealer again at surprising profit.

In less than two months we had sold and completely moved out of the Crestwood estate. I was surprised at how quickly the house sold. In fact it sold only four days after they put the for-sale sign in the yard. I was surprised but not disappointed; the estate always did seem a little bit much to me. I was never really all that comfortable there...maybe I had too many meager years to really enjoy the lap of luxury.

The apartment or condo as we now call it is cozy, spacious and plush with a great view of the city and I felt good about moving back to it. For Tamika it was a strategic common sense move, with the condo and Mercedes paid for, we would always have a comfortable place to live and a stylish car to drive. She envisioned our future in a home much more elegant than Crestwood and considered the Strathmore condo our comfortable little place in between.

We moved but Rhonda didn't. She stayed on as caretaker until the new owners arrived. She made things

so easy and comfortable the new owners hired her immediately upon their arrival.

On our last night in the Crestwood house we partied with Sam and Rhonda. It was our thank you dinner for Rhonda and neither she nor Sam knew it was our last day on Crestwood. To begin the evening we provided a limo and movie tickets for Rhonda and Sam. While they enjoyed a long limo ride and the latest blockbuster, Tamika and I cooked a delicious dinner.

Upon their return, we served drinks and joints in the formal living room. The mood was festive and loose.

Dinner, complete with vintage wine was served in the formal dining room while a professional piano player, hired for the night, played Rhonda's favorite selections. The room was filled with her favorite flowers and we both escorted Rhonda to her seat. On the table in front of her was a black marble plaque with a solid gold inscription that read, "We love you Rhonda. You fill a very special place and time in our lives that will always belong to just you. We thank you…for just being YOU. Love and kisses…Wint and T." Next to the plaque was the title to the Buick station wagon and next to that was a glowing letter of recommendation containing an offer of immediate employment with us anytime she wanted it. Under the letter was five thousand dollars in cash, severance pay. Tamika kissed Rhonda on her right cheek just as I kissed her on her left cheek then we hustled out to the kitchen to collect and serve the main course, leaving Sam to handle a shocked and sobbing Rhonda. After a few minutes I peeked out and they were slow dancing but Rhonda was still sobbing so we delayed dinner until they had set back down.

Rhonda was glowing, we had a great time at

dinner and afterwards toasted with some very, very old cognac and some primo weed. Everyone was feeling good when I remembered overhearing Rhonda tell a waitress at a party that someday she was gonna get naked and make love in that pool. So I suggested we all get naked and go for a swim. Within minutes we were all naked and splashing around in the swimming pool.

Inside the house the piano player continued to play. His melodies floated from the many speakers in the house and around the pool. Rhonda swam to the steps in the shallow end and lay back, within seconds Sam approached and entered her, she squealed and moaned loudly. Rhonda was completely lost in ecstasy as they fucked hard, the water slapping at their asses.

Tamika and I were watching, her titties bobbing on the water. From behind, I guided her to the steps and laid her next to Rhonda, raising her legs and entering her hot wet pussy. I winked at Sam and got on his rhythm as we fucked our women in unison while they wildly screamed and splashed the water. Watching Sam's dick slide in and out of Rhonda's fat wet pussy while my own rock hard dick was pumping in and out of Tamika was a trip. Suddenly Rhonda broke away from Sam and swam across the pool.

"Catch me if you can baby," she called to Sam. "Catch me and get all you want."

Sam chased Rhonda around then out of the pool.

"Catch me out here baby and I'll suck that good dick," she teased.

I picked up Tamika and walked up the steps out of the pool while trying to keep my dick in her. She was feeling good and bounced up and down, fucking me while I walked. I placed her gently on a lounge chair,

hooked her knees in my elbows and fucked her long and hard, while Sam lay on his back and Rhonda noisily sucked his dick. The sight and sound of them excited us and soon Tamika was grabbing me and gasping. I knew she was building an explosive climax and held back as long as I could. She grabbed me, slipped her legs around my back and sucked my dick with her pussy. It felt so goddamn good I thought I was gonna cry. We fucked with a new found smooth wet precision, fucking harder and faster while screaming, kissing and clutching each other. I came with such force it seemed to drive Tamika wild. She pumped hard then ground her pussy into me. I felt her contracting and twitching, while my dick continued to spasm and jerk for several moments. I stayed hard and we hung in afterglow, slowly fucking each other for several minutes before noticing that Rhonda and Sam had snuggled into a chaise lounge and were kissing and whispering.

"Ready to go home?" I asked Tamika.

"Yep and fuck all night long," she replied.

After several moments of trying, I eased my dick out of Tamika's sweet pussy and slowly we got up and dressed. Rhonda and Sam were surprised as we took them by the hand and lead them up to the Master Bedroom.

"We still have nine days left to live in this house and eight days before the remaining furniture is picked up," Tamika announced.

"We have already moved everything we are taking to the Strathmore and tonight was our last night on Crestwood," I added.

"We are leaving now and we want the two of you to totally and completely enjoy the estate for the

remaining days we have left," Tamika gushed.

"What?" Rhonda questioned, not believing her ears.

"Whoa...wait a minute now," Sam protested.

"No whoa or wait a minute to it, no what either, it is your estate for the next nine days," I explained. "Enjoy...See ya." I kissed Tamika and we ran from the house. Eager to move on, eager for the future and eager to get back to fucking each other.

Chapter eighteen

O*n the forty-seventh* of our self-imposed sixty day time limit the last sale was completed. Tamika settled all of our accounts and left the bank with a cashier's check for one hundred and seventy-five thousand dollars and a savings account balance of forty-one thousand, four hundred and ten dollars. I took the cashiers check to the lawyers' office, while at home Tamika completed all of the necessary income tax paper work, honestly reporting the sales made by check or electronic transfer and reporting only a tiny fraction of the sales made in cash. The purchase of our condo offset the gain we made on the sale of our house, but we owed a fair amount of taxes on the gain from the sale of the businesses. Tamika smiled, the tax bill was smaller than the savings account balance and the year was not over yet.

I left the lawyers office with an official document. The case had been dropped off the court's docket by a judge and the prosecuting attorney. Reasons: the case was deemed frivolous and lacking substantive evidence. To my understanding the word "frivolous" guarantees to

a ninety-nine percent certainty the case will never be tried. To date, no prosecutor has had the balls to attempt and try a case the court has deemed frivolous. I was stunned they were ready for me. The document spoke for itself. There was nothing for me to argue about and no reason to further insult the lawyers. I was disappointed with that but grudgingly satisfied over all, so I took the document home to Tamika.

When I returned to the condo Tamika was in the den. Her strongbox, ole promise number three was open and she was playing with the cash. She ran into my arms the minute she spotted me and squealed with delight when I gave her the document. She kissed me several times, kissed the document, danced around the room, then put the document into her fireproof file.

Again she danced around the den, stopping in front of me with a cold bottle of champagne and two glasses. I popped the cork, poured and we toasted her freedom, we toasted our love, we toasted our future, we toasted the whole bottle, before Tamika took my hand and lead me to ole promise number three. We sat down in front of it and Tamika giggled with excitement. "Winston...we did good! Real good, you will never guess how much we have left now that everything is settled," she challenged.

"I hope you are right about that did good part baby," I responded. "I'm still feeling the pain from what we just paid to those lawyers."

"Well forget the pain sweetheart, we have three hundred seventy-two thousand, nine hundred and eighty dollars here in unrecorded and unreported cash," she announced taking two big handfuls of cash and dropping it in my lap. Before long we were having a

money fight, laughing and rolling around in the money. Finally out of breath, Tamika set up and passionately kissed me, her eyes were sparkling like diamonds.

"Winston," she began, "Winston…I love you sweet Winston!" She got up, lit a joint and put it between my lips then got another cold bottle of champagne and sat back down. "The truth is Winston, that throughout my entire life I have always had you. As far back as I can remember whenever I was in trouble or feeling bad you were always there for me. You got me out of trouble and always made me feel good and feel good about myself. Now you have gotten me out of another jam that had I listened to you in the first place, I would have never gotten myself into."

"Oh yeah…what do you mean?" I asked.

"You remember when I first bought Flo's Beauty Shop you told me you thought keeping Florence Johnson was a bad move but I decided I needed to keep her. You were right, I should have cut her loose right from the git go," Tamika replied.

"Oh I don't know, hindsight is twenty-twenty. I really kinda think you are being too hard on yourself. You have accomplished one hell of a lot. In fact you have accomplished more in just a few years, than most folks including me have accomplished in a life time," I reassured her.

"If that's so it's only because I have you," Tamika responded. "I have always had you. I can do anything without fear or hesitation because I have you to run to if the shit gets deep. Now I'm going to do what I should have done in the first place and use your experience, your good common sense and your knowledge."

"Oh really?" I responded. "And just how you

gonna do that?"

"We never talked much about my beauty shops," she replied. "You gave me my space and I love you so much for doing that. I needed space then to prove myself and I did, several times over. Only one thing bothers me though and that is I know you were surprised to learn the Glory Hole Club was operating in each salon. I sincerely apologize Winston...and I love you. You were totally cool throughout this whole thing and I promise I will never blind-side you again. Starting right now, just like we talked on the lake, I am going to continue to talk out all of my business plans and moves with you first." She hopped up then placed a large snack tray, several joints and another bottle of champagne at my feet. She spread several pillows around me and sat back down with a large note pad in her hand. "Now that everything is sold and settled...we have no bills, no obligations and no responsibilities. We do have time, money and a lot of options...you know that sounds like an opportunity to think big. Maybe something major league," she suggested.

We talked through the remainder of that day and late into the night. The following day we slept late, went out to eat, took a walk, talked some more, made passionate love then fell asleep in each others arms.

Bright and early the next few mornings, Tamika was at her desk gathering information, drafting plans, and reviewing investment opportunities, while making calls and reservations. To get out of the condo for a while I went fishing and on the trip back I towed the boat and put it in our garage under the Strathmore. Then for several days we took life easy, cruised Bubba, visited with friends and ate in fine restaurants.

Finally, we secured Bubba in our garage next to the boat, activated the alarms on the condo and took a limo to the train station. In short order we settled into our private first class room aboard the Amtrak train.

In my opinion, first class on Amtrak is without question the best way to travel. I relaxed on the sofa and watched Tamika inspect and surprise herself with the many gadgets in our comfortable room. While watching her I remembered the frightening experience of driving her to the hospital to be born. Then thought about when she was just a baby wandering around the projects crying. I would find her and the second I made eye contact with her the crying would stop. Then when she got a little older, she was forever bothering me about wanting to watch my color TV. After she became a teenager who regularly flirted and seemed determined to tempt me, I considered her my little personal pain in the butt. But somewhere along the way she grew up and claimed what was hers from birth. I can't explain this woman and I'm scared to try.

The train lurched then slowing began moving out of the station. Tamika hugged me tightly then snuggled into my lap and me and Misses Littles settled in for some serious traveling and some serious loving. Love...excitement...expectation...and happiness. I must tell you, Tamika and I truly and deeply love each other. We are in love with each other. We love to talk, to touch, to kiss, to make love, to fuck, to be near each other, to be concerned for each other, to be proud, impressed, very happy and very, very satisfied with ourselves and with each other. Closed off from the world on this wonderful train, we celebrate and expand. We soar to new highs, elevating love making to a delicious art form!

"I love you Winston," Tamika whispered.

"I love you to, Tamika Littles," I replied as the train rounded a bend and picked up speed. We were naked and Tamika sat facing me, astride my lap with my dick inside her. The gentle rhythm of the train only intensified our already intense passion so for quite some time we slowly made love and watched the scenery roll by before an intense climax and lingering afterglow lured us both into deep peaceful sleep.

Eugene Rookwood's   *Trilogy of X*

Volume one -- **The X-Rated Deal**

The maturing of a young woman...in the arms of an older man...reluctantly provided by her sexy and street wise mother. The result of a risky x-rated deal that is poised to unravel but produces some unexpected and potentially explosive results.

Volume two -- **X and Complicated Rhythms**

Kenneth Weber is not sexually interested in his wife. His buddy, David Rollins, feels trapped and is ambivalent about his marriage, while Raymond Jenkins is certain his girlfriend is only a step better than a street whore. Marsha Weber has a dark sexual secret that drives her burning desires while Cyndi Rollins only want to be loved......For all of them, their raw honest needs ultimately forces drastic new experiences, relationships and outcomes...all in an effort to still the waters and uncomplicate the rhythms.

Volume three -- **Tamika – The Queen of X**

TOO HOT!!! for the screen... Available only in print!!

www.dexcelpublishing.com
Dexcel Publishing • P.O. Box 26586 • Indianapolis, IN 46226